THE
CHARACTERS
OF LOVE

THE
CHARACTERS
OF LOVE

Susie Boyt

Weidenfeld & Nicolson
LONDON

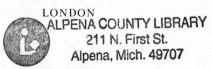

First published in Great Britain in 1996
by Weidenfeld & Nicolson

The Orion Publishing Group Ltd
Orion House
5 Upper Saint Martin's Lane
London WC2H 9EA

A catalogue record for this book is available
from the British Library

ISBN 0 297 81766 3

Typeset at The Spartan Press Ltd,
Lymington, Hants

Printed in Great Britain by
Butler & Tanner Ltd
Frome and London

For Tom

The quotation on page 10 is from Sandor Ferenczi's *Transitory Symptom Constructions during the Analysis, 1912*

Grateful acknowledgements is made to:

A. P. Watt Ltd on behalf of Michael Yeats for permission to print 'He Wishes for the Cloths of Heaven' from *The Collected Poems of W. B. Yeats*

Faber and Faber Ltd for 'In Memory of Sigmund Freud' from *Collected Poems* by W. H. Auden

Thames and Hudson, for quotation from *The Art of the Obvious* by Bruno Bettleheim and Alvin A. Rosenfeld, Great Britain (1993)

Chapter 1

It disgruntled Richard Fisher that he had not made more of his daughter, but he had justified it to himself by acknowledging he did not have a feeling for children and that this was a serious obstacle to their relation. He did not know how to go about liking children, just as he did not know how to make small talk with the man who cut his hair, or to feel sexually attracted to a red-headed woman. These were alien, unprecedented things for which he lacked a paradigm.

Fisher had known almost no children well. He was very familiar with several important cases, and from the studies he had read and the research he had witnessed, he liked to think he would be professionally equipped to handle a child who, for example had stopped talking as a reaction to exceptional circumstances in its life, its father beating its mother say, or the witnessing of some horrific accident, should the parents see fit to involve a psychiatrist. But he had never actually treated a child for more than a single session, fifty minutes in–out, the parents of such children generally preferring to consult a specialist.

Fisher knew there was an idea that play could be a useful tool in building up some sort of rapport between child and adult, but the world of play was one that he himself had little or no grasp of. The idea of rough and tumble, standing in goal between two discarded jumpers, using a slipper for a cricket bat, piggy-in-the-middle, Kerplunk, snap even, were not things with which he had ever had any dealings. There was a vast, red-and-yellow health centre in North London he had visited when assessing some student work as an external examiner, where sessions took place in an orange Wendy house and the sand pit and finger paints were employed in the treatment, but Fisher could not help but feel scorn for the sort of practitioners who favoured these methods, all be-linened Camden Town middle-aged divorcees rushing about like toddlers, pretending to be carefree children themselves, as if they hoped to set an example in this way. It wasn't exactly that this sort of approach felt undignified to him, although this certainly was part of it, but mainly he felt – it was hard to put his finger on it exactly – that it was an insult to the intelligence of the children. Exposing them to these hideously neurotic women for long periods of time, he was certain, could do the children no good and might actually do some harm. For the women it was a different story: generally it helped them enormously to have a new focus to carry them away from their obsessions with the painful, messy separations, the new romances that their husbands had embarked on, the distribution of the marital funds, and so on. But it was quite wrong for the children to be called upon as doctors when they had entered into the arrangement, quite specifically, as the patients. No amount of progressive game-playing could alter the fact. Fisher did occasionally like a game of chess and if he had had a teenage son he might have played chess with him, possibly; but he did not have a son, he had a daughter.

Fisher had read widely on the subject of children's development, but no one seemed to address the question of register. It seemed quite wrong to him to address a child as if it were more stupid than an adult, because generally this was not the case. Yet if you said to a child exactly what you would say to an adult of its class and interests and intelligence and preoccupations, frequently the conversation was unsatisfactory. In practice for instance, a friendly opener like, 'Suppose you tell me a little bit about yourself', or a less friendly way if it was late and one was tired: 'Now, what seems to be the problem?' or 'How can I help you?' did not work on children. Then, if you were lucky enough to draw the child out a bit, of course you had to get it to speak of worry rather than anxiety, of crushes, of hurt and sad and happy, but it was hard to get away from the fact that children lacked the articulacy and the vocabulary of the sort of cases at which Richard Fisher really excelled.

He was not a celebrity psychiatrist as such, but there was something in the make-up of the gifted adult, the dilemmas and strains faced by important men (and women), for which he felt a certain understanding. Fisher could count amongst his patients a former Cabinet minister, who at sixty-eight was finding himself disillusioned and prone to severe anxiety attacks. He had grown appalled at the new direction his party had taken and come to regard it as a haunting emblem of his own personal and moral decline. Fisher was also treating a top libel lawyer at the sound of whose name captains of industry and men of iron would quake. His discretion, intelligence and acute powers of observation gave him the appearance of having many layers of skin and secrets. He was a man used to playing his cards close to his chest, but very gradually the things that were troubling him were beginning to emerge: his sense of doubt and his occasional despair that his much-vaunted triumphs were hollow.

A Shakespearian actress, witty, blonde and masochistic, was another of Fisher's patients. She had been referred to him originally because of her habit of making small incisions in the skin of her legs and arms, beating her thighs until they were black and blue and pulling out her hair, and she wanted to give up the need for these abuses. A heart surgeon who suffered from depression, a lonely theologian, were also amongst the people who made their pilgrimages to 72 Wimpole Street. Although Fisher had been back in England for only six months following an eight-year stint in the United States, he had been able to build up this challenging and profitable practice with the help of some of his doctor friends, who confidently referred their nervous patients to his care.

This specialization was a new departure for Fisher, who had begun his career in the outpatients clinic of a large London teaching hospital, where the patients he faced were as hindered by social issues such as unemployment and homelessness as they were by depression and other mental imbalance. A large part of his job, therefore, had little or nothing to do with the practice of psychiatry. Their needs were immediate and keen and as his brief was to treat each patient for a maximum of four sessions, his aspirations for their mental health were forced to remain at the lower end of the scale. Largely it had been a sticking-plaster service he offered: he provided practical help and advice about benefits and rights, housing, night shelters and so on, information so central to the wellbeing of his patients that he had made a study of the system on their behalf; he also relied heavily on medication. The short-term results of the prescription of certain drugs were often enough to get a patient back on his feet again, give him the confidence and the strength to find accommodation and employment and in some cases many of the symptoms of depression fell away with the resolution of practical difficulties.

Fisher had left the hospital after six years when a research post at an American university had become available. This coincided with professional difficulties in London. The psychiatric wing in which he worked had witnessed four suicides in three months and although the following inquiry had not exactly blamed the department, the general morale of the unit was extremely low.

Fisher's disillusionment with psychiatry and his slow seduction by psychoanalysis had begun almost as soon as he arrived in America. Initially it had appealed to the perfectionist in him. It seemed, for the patient, the manner of living most likely to produce the fullest life. He liked the sky-high daring of its aspirations and, having witnessed the research and clinical findings of some of America's most eminent practitioners, he regularly saw the awareness and potential of patients expanding to the richest and most infinite degree, and the daily effects of this were exceptional capacity for choice, achievement, courage and love. More and more, traditional psychiatry took on a dingy aura for Fisher; it seemed cowardly and rooted in a concern to keep a man ticking over, but nothing more, unhappy, but not unhappy enough to force a break with the emotion.

In his new premises in Wimpole Street, despite amazing developments in the manufacture of drugs (the subtleties of the new antidepressants, in particular, really interested him), Fisher found that he was resorting to his prescription pad less and less. The treatment he now offered had become a talk-based therapy.

Fisher had not seen his daughter for quite some time, not since his return from America, in fact. Days before his departure all those years ago, Nell's mother, in a long and vituperative letter, had made it quite clear that in future he would be unwelcome in the household, that any attempt at contact would be a harmful disruption to what was already an oversensitive childhood and that for all concerned it was far better that he stayed away. It was arranged that a sum of money would be credited to her account at three-monthly intervals without any contact having to be made. She had also insisted on changing her daughter's surname (with her own) back to her maiden name, Dorney. Fisher had deferred to her wishes absolutely in this instance, although it was hard to think of a case when he had done so before, but if his reasons now were more selfish than considerate, it was not something that kept him awake at night. Leaving England after a brief failed marriage (the failure, in his eyes, being entirely his own fault), with his confidence at an uncharacteristic low and virtually no liking for himself, his estranged wife's wishes did not seem unreasonable.

It was only once he had reached the United States, when he had thought in depth about the person he had become and been able to say stiffly, 'Come on man, this just won't do', that effecting any kind of change in himself seemed at all possible. There and then he had sat down and drawn up a moral inventory in which he catalogued all his professional and personal failings and considered ways in which he could improve. The question of Nell needled him slightly, but he felt it to be of paramount importance, having treated his wife rather roughly, rather shabbily, that he obeyed her keenly delivered instructions to the letter. The idea of Nell he situated at the very back of his mind and there she remained quietly, occasionally stirring his curiosity, but only in the vaguest and most abstract way.

One spring Monday morning at ten past nine Fisher sat reading in his consulting room. The scuffed red-leather seat, that had been his father's, was positioned a few feet away from the large, oak doctor's desk and Fisher leaned hard into the arc of the chair back so that it rested against the wall directly behind. He placed his legs, crossed at the feet, on top of the leather surface of the desk.

Having recently decided that his block with children was a form of weakness, an unnecessary professional shortcoming that needed remedying, he had told his doctor friends that he would be very interested in treating a child. Amy, the nine-year-old daughter of an American businessman, was due at ten. All Fisher knew about her was that her mother was dead and that she and her father lived together in St John's Wood.

After a while, Fisher got up, went over to his couch and lay down. He straightened his long legs so that the toes of his shoes peeped an inch or two over the edge. He let out a sigh and continued with his book.

In your own first encounter with the patient you will perceive far more than you can possibly register consciously. How does this boy look? How is he dressed? Do his clothes look like ones he's selected himself? How does he walk? Has he brought along a special toy? If so, what is it? Does he play with the

*toys in your playroom or simply look at them? Is he interacting
with his parents in the waiting room, or is he playing alone in
the corner?*

As far as Amy was concerned, Fisher had resolved to
invest considerable effort and study into treating her
effectively. It was likely that a large amount could be
learned from her. Fisher plunged himself into case
studies and research findings for the three weeks in
which he anticipated her appointment. He was quietly
curious about children. They seemed like another
species to him. His experience in America, he felt,
especially suited him to be Amy's doctor, should the
Anglo-American dislocation theme enter into their
discourse. Fisher's good intentions towards the child
meant making concessions to all aspects of her contact
with him and that included the waiting room: the week
of her first appointment he had added to his usual
magazine order of *Vogue*, *Harper's*, the *New Yorker*, the
Spectator, *The Economist*, *Good Housekeeping*, *Radio* and *TV
Times*, several comics including two American titles, to
make her feel at home. He had sent his secretary out in
her lunch hour to Hamley's to buy toys for a girl and
she had returned with a doll, a teddy bear, a little craft
set where you used a red plastic cotton reel with four
pins in the top as a sort of knitting machine, a set of
jacks with a red bouncy ball and a game of draughts.
She had also bought tissues printed with Walt Disney
characters in case the child should feel the need to cry,
some packets of Smarties and a bottle of orange squash.

Fisher opened the window a little to make the room seem fresher and more inviting. He placed the toys in a wicker basket in a corner of the consulting room, the box of tissues he positioned on the low table that sat between his chair and the chair on which she would sit. He imagined the child would not wish to lie down on the couch. It was ten to ten. Fisher buzzed through to his secretary on the intercom, 'Mrs Summers, has the child arrived yet? . . . Well, when she does, could you let me know straight away. Thanks very much.' Fisher picked up his book again and read:

> *Many intelligent children at the stage of repression marked by the latency period, before they have gone through 'the great intimidation', regard adults as dangerous fools, to whom one cannot tell the truth without running the risk of being punished for it: and whose inconsistencies and follies have to be taken into consideration. In this children are not so very wrong.*

It was almost ten o'clock. Fisher rang through again, 'Still no sign?' This annoyed him. If an adult was late it was reasonably straightforward: he would simply receive a shorter session, much of which might well be concerned with the hostility that had caused the patient to lose the time in the first place. But it was different in the case of children, who generally did not manage their own travel arrangements. While he waited, Fisher drifted off into a series of musings.

Psychoanalysis had distinctly heroic qualities for Fisher. In a mild, English fashion, he was extremely proud to be involved in this discipline neatly situated between science and art, which concerned itself with the bringing about of personal revolutions. Fisher had carried throughout his psychoanalytic training in America a conviction that the profession he was apprenticed to, when practised properly, was the finest in the world. A simple belief lay at the heart of Fisher's faith: a firm psychoanalytic alliance could facilitate the shedding of unhappiness. If a patient compelled himself to assume roles and practices that made him miserable, it was the analyst's job to help him to take them off. There might not be obvious consolations under all the cleverly constructed despairings, but there was always something that more closely resembled what was true.

Poetry had been written, great poetry, about the aims of this practice and it was doubtful if the same could be said for the other method. Auden's poem about Freud, for instance, Fisher had by heart.

> *He wasn't clever at all: he merely told*
> *The unhappy Present to recite the Past*
> *Like a poetry lesson till sooner*
> *Or later it faltered at the line where*
>
> *Long ago the accusations had begun,*

Fisher especially liked 'wasn't clever at all'. It made him laugh. In time, Fisher realized that psychiatry had things to offer him also, that in certain cases, a course of prescribed drugs could help with the initial building of the therapeutic alliance, if the patient was too depressed to attend his sessions, say, or had extreme behavioural difficulties that medication could balance and check.

People that Fisher admired had misgivings about the profession, chiefly that psychoanalysis was unsuited to the lifespan. He had known of many many cases where the treatment had exceeded ten years, which certainly was an enormous commitment. Yet if the patient desired to unlearn the lifetime of excuses, rectitude and overfamiliar gestures which had led him to seek treatment in the first place, was it unreasonable to imagine that the unlearning of these now unwanted, but still firmly clung-to habits, might take up as much time as the original learning of them had done, if not longer? Some patterns of behaviour human beings compelled themselves into had been learned or taught so young and for so many years that they were almost impossible to forget, like riding a bicycle. That there was a method that could aid this forgetting, that one could forge one's career out of it, for these facts Fisher was supremely grateful.

Fisher rang through to Mrs Summers again. It was ten-fifteen. Amy had not materialized. It was unusual for Fisher to feel anxious, but this is what he found himself feeling as he put down the book that lay slackly in his hands. Then, after a few moments, the anxiety cleared and focused his mind in a way that took him wholly by surprise. He was curious to discover himself thinking of another little girl whose existence for him was hazy. He pictured a red-faced, white-haired roly-poly child with falling-down nappy and runny nose and suddenly his interest was aroused more powerfully than it had occurred to him would be possible over something relating to his former life. 'I know. Why don't I go and see her?' he suddenly found himself saying out loud and the very words seemed to bring a smile into his voice. 'I'll go and see Nell, that's what I'll do. Why didn't I think of it before?'

Chapter 2

Nell and Laura had been best friends ever since Catherine Parker had gone off with Kate Monkhouse in the first year juniors. Arriving at school one morning, Nell found a note from Catherine stuck to her desk with pink bubble gum.

Dear Nell,
Me and Kate are going to be best friends, so we will have to break up. Sorry, Luv Catherine. PS I need my Ella tape back.

By morning break the news was round the school. Nell was seen grinning in netball but people speculated that underneath she was gutted like a fish. By lunchtime quite a band of sympathizers and gossip mongers were surrounding Nell when she reached into her coat pocket and therein found a piece of folded yellow notepaper that read:

Dear Nell,
Can we be best friends? I like your hair and you are top in English, love Laura.

Nell wrote back immediately.

Dear Laura,
Yes Yes Yes, love Nell. PS YES

After that Nell and Laura were always together. Most evenings they played at each other's houses after school, watching TV together, doing their homework together and writing plays, which they performed for their mothers at weekends, Laura a batty gym teacher: 'Now then girls, there's only a mile to go, half a mile if you hurry'; to Nell's formidable headmistress: 'Girls! Girls! Cease this vulgar brawl at once!' When they were eight, one night after watching an episode of *Dallas* in their pyjamas, they practised on each other through six layers of cling film the French kissing they had witnessed on screen. Some weeks later, disillusioned with their mothers, they packed twenty sandwiches and their wellington boots into a rucksack and ran away to Regent's Park, where they remained for two hours before returning home bloated from the bread and ham and blue with cold. When they were nine Nell found a twenty-pound note in the street and they blew it all on the Pick'n'Mix at Woolworth's, each girl dragging home a large carrier bag brimming with boiled sweets and fun-size chocolate bars. When they were eleven Laura sent Nell a postcard from Spain:

Kissed a boy in a disco last night. He was called Miguel.
What a nightmare. Love Laura

'*Dear Laura*,' Nell wrote back. '*That's me gel!*'

When they were thirteen they took themselves off to a hairdresser's behind Oxford Circus and came home flaunting tiny rolled-gold sleepers in their beetroot-red ears.

Laura lived with her mother and younger brother Mathew in a large terraced house off Camden Square and Nell lived with her mother in a smaller, dingier house, four streets away.

Laura's father lived in America and sent for her every school holiday. His fatherly qualities were legendary. He FedExed Laura and Mathew presents from Disney shops. He sent them tickets to visit him, met them at the airport with a huge sign he had painted himself saying, AMERICA WELCOMES LAURA AND MATHEW NESBITT. He would run to meet them at the barrier with open arms and money jangling loudly in his pockets. He called Laura 'Little Miss'. They had crisp, chewy waffles with maple syrup and cinnamon toast at the Saint Regis; they took trips to the World Trade Center just as the sun was setting; they ate sushi in sky scraper restaurants. They got returns for the matinée of *Guys and Dolls* and afterwards bought white jeans and sneakers and sang the tunes from the show as they played frisbee in Central Park. They ordered pizza from room service and root beer. When they flew on planes together they would eschew the airline dinners and eat the hunks of bread and salami and strawberries and Swiss cheese that he had bought at Dean and DeLuca. He took Laura and Mathew to see his orthodontist and now they had regular, American-style teeth. He taught her to say, 'When I eat beigel I think Heigel.' He had a photo of the three of them taken together and presented it to her in a chunky silver frame.

Nell's father never sent for her. Nell's mother asked Laura's mother if Laura could kindly not mention these trips to Nell; she hadn't shown any signs, as yet, but it must get to her. But Laura and Nell had already decided that Nell's father was dead.

Nell's father was a mystery. The words 'My Father' when positioned inside a question, Nell had learned, gave her power and would, like a dangerous form of play, climbing and jumping, say, have supplied her with a weapon to use against her mother had she desired one. For the very mention of the words 'My Father' caused her mother's face to contort, her features would appear to gather into the middle of her face, her breathing would quicken and her voice would sound straitened and like ice. All this (at the same time as a supreme effort towards nonchalance on her mother's part) was excruciating to witness and Nell experienced it, on the very few occasions when she had asked, as a huge deterrent to enquiry.

Nell harboured one memory of her father. It was when Nell had been going through the terrible twos, soon after Fisher had moved out of the family home. He had called round apparently one afternoon to sort out some business with her mother and caught Nell in the middle of a vehement temper tantrum. As she lay on the floor kicking her legs in the air and pounding the ground with her fists and screeching, Fisher had looked at her with distaste and said to her mother, 'Can nothing be done about that child?'

Once or twice Nell's mother had cobbled together some further explanations for Fisher's vanishing act.

We had an enormous row when you were one and he decided to try his luck in America. He took all his stuff on a great big boat. I asked him not to contact me and he agreed to respect my wishes.

No, I don't have an address for him. We didn't ever bother with a divorce, so, I suppose, yes, in the eyes of the law we are still married, if he's still alive, that is.

No, it's not impossible that he could be dead and lying at the bottom of the sea, although highly unlikely. What made you think of that darling? I certainly wouldn't dwell on it if I were you.

These different stories chimed and jarred to Nell like snatches of song, half sea shanty, half nursery rhyme.

> *Oh, when I was one my mother and father*
> *Had an enormous row*
> *My father sailed to America*
> *And that's where he'd be now.*
> *But the ship it tossed him this way that way*
> *Over the Irish sea*
> *It struck a plank and then it sank*
> *Down into the Bri-nee.*

'When I grow up I think I might make a visit to my father's grave,' Nell told her mother. Her mother rubbed her hand across her forehead and up and down the right side of her face, finally making a shelf of her fist on which to rest her chin. She sighed, 'Oh Nell, shush.'

After that Nell started saying that she didn't have a dad. She had no picture in a frame, no airplane food and trips to Martha's Vineyard, no costly orthodontics to prove that he had ever existed.

'You must have one.'

'No. I think I had one for a bit, but no, you don't need one really. And anyway, we were never specially fond of each other.' Or, on another occasion:

'My mother made me out of her tummy on her own.'

'You sure?'

'Positive.' Nell knew what sex was. Fuck was a rude word for making love ... making love was a soppy word for sex ... sex was an abbreviation for sexual intercourse ... sexual intercourse was when a man inserted his penis into a woman's vagina. At ten the girls in the 4C were given a talk on contraception.

'I don't know why they bother. We probably know more than they do, anyway,' Laura said.

'It makes them feel better,' Nell said. 'I suppose we better humour them.'

'Yeah,' said Chloe, a tall girl who already had a boyfriend.

The fat woman in the Virgin-Mary-blue uniform began. She had been the school nurse for as long as anybody could remember, making regular visits to check the children's sight and hearing and to search their heads for lice. Since completing a six-week course at a training centre near Boreham Wood, she now taught health education and CSP (Careers, Social and Personal). In her earlier incarnation Nell had once had a run-in with her for being cheeky.

Nell: If nits like clean hair are you implying I've got dirty hair because there aren't any nits, or what?

Nit lady: ['Bing' went the nit comb on Nell's head.] If you haven't got anything sensible to say, keep quiet madam.

'Now, I imagine it will be some time before you find boyfriends and decide to have or not to have intercourse, but it's important to know about contraception in order to prevent pregnancy.' She drew a condom in a silver foil package out of her handbag, she took a diaphragm out of its blue plastic case and placed it on the table, then she took a metal strip of pills and put these down on the table also. She talked about this array of apparatus, mentioning from time to time, 'The only way to avoid pregnancy altogether is to make sure that no intercourse takes place.'

'Surprise, surprise,' Chloe said out loud. A few girls laughed.

'However, if and when you and your partner feel ready for sex these are the most popular ways of preventing conception.' She took the condom out of its packet and stretched and twanged it. Twenty ten- and eleven-year-olds laughed. The lady handed each girl a pamphlet and closed the discussion with a brief talk about acne.

Nell read the pamphlet. The writers seemed almost certain that to have a baby a woman needed to have sexual intercourse with a man. She read the pamphlet several times. She had been labouring under a misconception. It wasn't just her and her mother. At one stage a third party must have been involved.

Nell's eleventh birthday fell two weeks after this and her mother invited all the little girls from her class to attend. Twenty small girls sat eating cup cakes, out of which circles of sponge had been scooped, the cavities had been filled with pink icing and the removed portion split and stuck back in at jaunty angles to resemble butterfly wings. There were sausage rolls, rust-coloured prawn cocktail crisps, bread and butter covered in rainbow sprinkles, chocolate Viscount biscuits wrapped in green and orange damasked foil and little tarts filled with garish red jam and fluorescent lemon curd. The twenty-four girls passed the parcel, played musical statues, pinned the tail on the donkey. Then it was time for the cake.

'*Happy Birthday to me, Arrivederci,*' sang Nell.

'*Happy Birthday to you, Squashed tomatoes and stew,*' sang the guests.

'*Happy Birthday Dear Nell,*' sang the man who was standing at the back of the room, an early father coming to collect his daughter, '*Happy Birthday to you.*'

Nell's mother was in a fluster slicing up the cake, stopping now and then to push up the sleeve of her jersey which kept dangling into the icing. She was concentrating hard, putting her whole arm into the slicing of each piece, the action beginning with a tensing of the shoulder muscle, as if she were carving a tough piece of meat. She folded each portion in a red paper napkin, occasionally stopping to make calculations to ensure that every child would get one. She was all fingers and thumbs and was making a mess of the job, cutting some pieces that were so small that they crumbled in her hands and others that were great doorsteps and had to be sandwiched together with two napkins. Nell saw the man watching her mother, her face and her arms flushed pink, hacking up the cake in this rough manner. The job completed, she left the room hurriedly. Nell began distributing the red parcels, awarding the largest pieces to the girls she liked most. Laura's bit was a small brick. When all the girls had been given some, Nell handed a piece to the man who was waiting.

'And I've got something for you,' he said and bent down to pick up a large rectangular box that lay at his feet.

The box was covered in pink paper printed with gold and silver stars. 'How nice,' Nell said and opened it up.

Inside the box was a white box and inside this box was a dress, and what a dress. There was an underskirt made of crisp white silky material, many stiff and fluffy layers that were almost see-through, and the dress itself was short-sleeved, calf-length white satin, with pairs of blue and white birds delicately embroidered all over the fabric. At the back hung a heavy blue satin sash and Nell counted twenty-four blue silk-covered buttons.

Nell looked at it and held it up against her body dressed in pale pink corduroy trousers and silver crocheted cardigan. It was what a rich person's well-dressed doll would wear. 'How nice,' said Nell. 'How very, very nice.'

The man smiled and stammered something about 'Little girls . . . ' that trailed away into nothing.

Her mother started talking, 'Nell darling, isn't it beautiful? Look at those lovely birds. Some old lady must have sat up night after night embroidering them.'

'Or some old man,' piped up Nell.

When everyone had left, Nell put the dress back in the boxes and laid it on her bed, looking in on it, lifting the lid every so often, the way one might check up on a baby.

'Do you think you could wear it?' her mother asked doubtfully.

'Well, it's not exactly me,' Nell said. 'And it is a bit of an eyesore, let's face it.'

'Nell!'

Money was tight at that time and after much umming and ahhing between the two of them, Nell's mother returned the dress to the shop in Bond Street. The huge white marble showroom sold not only children's clothes but high-class household items such as monogrammed powder-blue linen sheets and thick white towels that were six foot deep and eight foot wide. The flurry of assistants were dignified and polite. The dress had cost £340. They suggested alternative garments for some time: a silky halter-neck floral swimsuit, a quilted mauve satin dressing gown with matching high-heeled fluffy mauve mules, which were right up Nell's street, but Nell's mother held out for cash. Pocketing the wad of twenty-pound notes she went straight to the post office to pay the gas and electric bills.

Then she drifted down Oxford Street to see what she could see. She entered a large department store and headed up to the children's department, where she bought two pairs of shoes, one for school and one black patent pair for parties. Then she bought a red tracksuit with two white stripes down the leg, a new school blazer and a box-pleated navy blue school skirt (Nell had almost grown out of her current one), and then a nightdress and three pairs of blue woollen tights for winter. A matronly shop assistant insisted on trotting behind her carrying the purchases and her stooped back and considerable number of years finally obliged Nell's mother to end the shopping spree. Laden with carrier bags, and the bag with the two sharp-cornered boxes of shoes in it bit and chafed against her leg, she headed to St Martin's Lane and bought Nell a white tutu from a ballet shop – it had all the festiveness of the original dress, with none of the unpalatable bits – and two wrap-around ballet tops in pink and powder blue. She headed up towards Rupert Street market, where she bought Nell a pair of red jeans and a dark green and blue mini kilt and a long-sleeved white T-shirt with a red heart on it. She could carry no more, but she did not want to waste money on a taxi, and although she could barely walk with all the shopping that she had, she gathered it all up and slumped herself and the things onto the bus. Once home, she began a mammoth wrapping operation so that it would all be ready when Laura's mother dropped Nell back from school.

Nell was delighted with the stack of goods: 'Something for every occasion.' She tried on all the garments in a variety of combinations: tutu and blazer, nightdress and kilt. She put a record on and then paraded round the kitchen giving a fashion show to her mother, who applauded and cheered at every outfit, taking a hundred pictures with a camera that gave off a huge flash but unfortunately had no film in it. She gave Nell a cocktail glass full of orange juice as a prop and a cigarette holder, then fetched her a pair of her way-too-big high heels to wear. But when it was time for bed, and Nell arranged all the new things in her cupboard, including the gold and silver box that had contained the dress, for no reason at all, she started to cry. 'You're probably just exhausted after all that,' her mother said. But Nell simply could not stop crying and although she said to her mother that it was nothing, what she felt in her heart was that somehow something completely bad had taken place. Finally she did manage to stop herself for a few moments and her mother went happily off to bed while Nell, in a renewed surge of grief, wept into her pillow, 'I want the dress, I want the dress back, I waa-aa-aant the dre-ee-eess ba-aa-aack.' And as she cried she felt as if she had experienced a loss of infinite proportions. The dress was gone for ever. She struck a blow to her head with her little fist as a punishment for being so stupid. It had only just occurred to her that the man was her father.

Next day Nell said she was too ill to go to school, and the next day, and the next. The day after that a postcard came for Nell from the man. It was printed with his name and number and an address in Wimpole Street.

Dear Nell,

It was very good to see you on your birthday. Perhaps you would come and have tea with me, this time, on Wednesday afternoon between five and six-thirty and, if it would suit, on subsequent Wednesdays at that time. You might telephone and leave a message with my secretary if this is inconvenient. If someone can bring you here I will see that you get home.

Best, Richard.

Nell's illness cleared up the next day, which was a relief to her mother, and the two of them began to brace themselves for the visit. 'Will he expect to see me in the dress?' Nell asked anxiously.

'No, darling, because you'll be going from school and will be in your uniform.'

Mrs Dorney dropped Nell off at exactly five o'clock at the shiny dark wooden door near Marylebone Road. It was an enormous house with six or seven floors. There were eight bells and the bottom one read 'Richard Fisher'. Once pressed, the brass button gave off such a huge buzzing sound that Nell jumped back and by the time she had found her footing on the broad stone step, given her head a sharp rap with the edge of her knuckle for being so clumsy and recomposed herself, Richard Fisher was looking down at her from the doorway. He towered above her, his six foot four lengthened by the pinstriped fabric of his suit. 'How lovely to see you,' he said. 'Please come in.'

They walked from the small, square hall down a corridor and through a heavy white door with many locks on it into a large rectangular sitting room containing seven or eight armchairs, a floral sofa, a fireplace with a basket of dried flowers positioned in the grate and a square table covered in magazines. Nell took a seat and he disappeared into a room and came back with a tray containing a plate of sandwiches, a beaker of orange squash and two sachets of fruit cake, like those bought on trains. He disappeared again and returned with a basket containing various toys and games.

'I don't know if any of these things might be of interest,' he said.

'Thank you.' Nell noticed that the toys in the basket were brand new. She opened the box containing a child's knitting set and, reading the instructions, she started looping and fastening red wool round the little pins on the Knitting Nancy, which looked like an oversized red cotton reel with stubby spokes sticking up on it. Before long she had built up quite a momentum. Richard Fisher watched intently; she seemed quite absorbed in her task and so he ate a sandwich and then picked up his newspaper and started reading.

They had been sitting reading and knitting like some old married couple for quite some time, but when Nell looked up at the clock on the mantelpiece she saw to her dismay that it was only five-thirteen. She put down her knitting on the arm of her chair and the long tube of red wool she had made lolled over the edge like a tongue. Fisher saw this and immediately laid down his paper and offered her a sandwich and a small tea plate on which to put it. Nell took the plate and looked round the room. She was struck by how tidy it was. There were virtually no things in it, no photographs, pictures, little ornaments, letters, mess, nothing, not even a radio, a television or a forgotten cup or scrap of lint on the carpet, not any books even. She took a bite out of the sandwich. It tasted very cold. 'Is this sandwich bought from a shop?' she asked, surprised, impressed.

'Yes, I'm afraid you must forgive me. I've been in an awful hurry all day, so I had to send out for a few bits and pieces. My secretary bought them at Boots. Perhaps next time we'll go and choose something together. There's rather a good delicatessen in Marylebone High Street. You see, I don't know what you like.'

'Oh, I like everything,' she said.

'When I was your age, I would practically eat the pattern off the plate,' he told her.

'Were you very fat, then?'

'No,' he said. 'No, I wasn't. We ran around a lot at home.'

'In London?'

'In Wiltshire. The house had a small park and some farm land.'

'Oh,' she said.

'Do you prefer town or country?' he asked Nell.

'I haven't been in the country much. We went to Devon for our school journey in the third years, up in Dawlish, near Teignmouth. I liked it, but there's this girl in our class called Smelly and the other girls in her room complained that she was too messy and they always got low marks in inspection and so the teachers said she had to move to a separate annexe on her own on the other side of the courtyard and every night she screamed and cried because she couldn't get to sleep and she was scared of the dark and so in the end I told her to come and sleep in my bed, but I couldn't sleep because of the smell and in the morning when we had showers I washed her from head to toe, but the smell wouldn't go away. I suppose it must have been on her clothes. I did wash some of them as well, but I couldn't wash them all because I didn't want to hurt her feelings. It was awful.'

'It sounds awful.'

'I don't know what the teachers were thinking of, putting her on her own miles away from anyone. I got really cross about it. I phoned up Mum to complain to the headmistress, but nothing really happened. It was funny though. The next day I washed her again. We made it into a sort of game. We both washed for ages. We were bright pink. I thought if the smell went away people wouldn't call her Smelly any more.'

Vastly embarrassed and almost out of breath, Nell stopped talking. She could have kicked herself. She thought of the two-year-old kicking her legs and screaming so disgustingly, all out of control. Fisher seemed to be thinking over what she had said.

'And this girl, are you still friendly with her?'

'Not really. She doesn't come to school much. She's got something wrong with her insides, she had to go into hospital, to have an operation. Some of the boys in our class say that, that she had to have an abortion and it went wrong. I don't know though.'

'How old is she?'

'Eleven.'

Nell fell silent. After a short while she resumed her knitting and Fisher picked up the paper again. He ate some more sandwiches and opened up one of the sachets of cake and put it on a plate for her. She ate it up slowly, leaving one currant on the plate. It was almost six-thirty now. There were five minutes left and the impending separation was making Nell feel nervous, not least because she had failed to thank her father for the dress and she was becoming increasingly anxious about how to broach the subject.

At six-thirty the buzzer sounded.

'I suppose we ought to see about getting you home,' said Richard Fisher. 'Two minutes,' he muttered to the person at the door through the entryphone.

Fisher gathered up his newspaper and picked up his briefcase, helped Nell into her new blazer, which she had taken off and hidden behind her chair on arrival, and then they were outside on the doorstep and he was locking a number of heavy locks with silver keys. A black taxi was waiting for them and while its engine gurgled and shuddered, Fisher held the door of the cab open for her and she clambered in and sat down on one of the tip-up seats, and then he hopped in and sat down opposite her, stretching out his stripey legs. He gave her address to the driver, adding, 'And then to Grosvenor Square.' In the cab Fisher glanced through the newspaper and Nell wound up her watch until it wouldn't wind any more. When they drew up at her mother's house Fisher said, 'See you next week at the same time,' and Nell said, 'Thank you very much.' 'Do you need anything?' he asked her as she climbed out of the taxi, but it was too late. The taxi had already driven off.

Alone in the taxi, Fisher was surprised to find himself intrigued by the child. Her small, dark figure, her confidence, her liveliness – it had all caught him unawares, and the result was a new and nameless pleasurable emotion. Nell had seemed to her father nicely compact, pleasingly self-contained – even while spilling out the story of the child who stank, when all he had asked her was whether she liked the country. She was obviously a metropolitan creature with a modern city bearing and London manners; generally he liked children to seem and look more old-fashioned, unexposed to anything as garish as trying to soap the smell of urine from a slum child. But he had liked the way she had applied herself to the little knitting game and the story about the other child had shown her instincts to be rather delicately feminine. It worried Fisher that she attended the kind of school where such a regrettable incident should have occurred. Of course, he had no wish to interfere – the mother was obviously doing a good enough job – but mightn't she be better off in a, well, a more academic environment? She was obviously intelligent, and if all parties agreed, why shouldn't he come up with such moneys as would be necessary? His old school had gone Co-ed. He could take her up there to have a look round. Then she could concentrate on her education rather than administering to the needs of her fellow pupils all the time. Although she was certainly healthy and robust, a child ought to breathe fresh air, to go riding, to see cows being milked, to swim in the sea, not to be cooped up in the city for months on end with only the occasional traumatic trip to the West Country to put roses in its cheeks, surely Jane would agree to that?

His own childhood in Wiltshire had been character-ized by vast amounts of physical exercise which had made him the tower of strength that he was today. He prided himself on the fact that, apart from a bout of measles when he was seven, he had never had a single day of illness in his life.

Once home, Fisher gathered the many letters that lay waiting for him on the door mat and took them to his study, where he eased himself into his chair and picked up the newspaper again, but after a few moments his eyes wandered onto the pile of unopened envelopes. Perhaps he ought to make a start on them, get them over and done with so that he could relax before his dinner date. He reached absently inside the first envelope but its contents made him sit bolt upright in his chair.

Dear Fisher, (it began)
How grossly unfair you are, flexing your professional muscles at me in this way.

The letter came from a colleague and former friend of Fisher's with whom he was conducting a rather public argument. Indeed their recent falling out over professional differences had become well known amongst their circle, thanks to the friend's sense of outrage and injury, which he had not kept to himself. Having written a book of psychoanalytic essays from a clinical perspective, the friend, Doctor Alexander Phelps (both he and Fisher were in the small minority of analysts who believed that all practitioners should undergo medical training), had embarked on a garish, large-scale publicity campaign which had not only taken in several double-page spreads in Sunday supplements, but also two television appearances, one on a breakfast show alongside Barbara Cartland who was promoting her biography, and one on a late-night arts programme where he sat on a panel of artists and writers who were assessing the retrospective of a major twentieth-century figurative painter. Although the book had been written with an audience well versed in psychoanalytic theory in mind, it had been jauntily and provocatively presented (its cover resembling that of a popular novel) and was being marketed as a general interest title.

The argument that had occasioned the rift stemmed from Fisher's contempt, not for the book which he found challenging and of some interest, but for the high profile its writer seemed to be seeking through it, which he perceived as not merely cheap, but a lamentable professional error. Firstly, Phelps's recent activities seemed to call his seriousness, and by extension the seriousness of the profession, into question: surely there were tasks that ought to be more pressing to him than the whiling away of hours answering questions from banal journalists, getting himself plastered all over the papers? Let the book be extracted, certainly, thought Fisher, issue a brief statement, or even a little interview with a serious, interested party, but posing for numerous photos on an assortment of *chaises-longues*, including one that had been covered in a fabric printed with busts of Freud himself, that was going too far. Secondly, it seemed vastly discourteous to his patients to put himself forward in this way, to Fisher's mind, and might easily interfere with the process of transference, which was one that he and Phelps had formerly agreed to be their most important tool. Thirdly, that Phelps was obviously stimulated by all the fuss that was being created around him struck Fisher as vastly disappointing in a man whose unswerving dedication to his profession had been an example to him throughout his own career.

After some time Fisher had written his friend a stiff letter to this effect, and Phelps's letter of justification now lay in his hands. It continued:

Your complete failure to understand the kind of work that my words have to do comes as a bitter disappointment to me. As you have an intellect that I have greatly admired in the past, I can only attribute your misunderstanding to an act of will.

His defence of his own behaviour centred round his belief in the need, in the light of the bad publicity that surrounded psychoanalysis and talk-based therapies at the moment, to champion genuine, accomplished, psychoanalytic psychotherapy, that which had been invented by Freud and took into account all the developments which had since occurred, a therapy conducted by a small body of highly trained profes-sional practitioners, who had not only qualified as medical doctors, but were steeped in the history of literature and ideas, in myth and archaeology, music, theology, fine art, linguistics, the law, social policy and administration, as well as having undergone a rigorous psychoanalytic training. To have the chance to state his point of view to a wide audience it was worth the mildly compromising photographs, and as for the slight discomfort his patients might initially feel at his exposure, at his (and here he quoted from Fisher's letter) having made himself 'public property', this would soon die down and might even serve a useful function in itself. After all, anything that was brought to the session had value.

Fisher's opinion was not greatly altered by reading the letter, but he enjoyed and was impressed by the definition of psychoanalysis put forward by his friend. The list of accomplishments struck him, as far as form was concerned, as not unlike something he had read in a Jane Austen novel describing what a young lady should be. Fisher briefly enjoyed the idea of telling Phelps that he was almost surprised that a degree of proficiency at singing and the pianoforte had not been included. Although the letter did not dispel his doubts about his friend's practices, it focused Fisher's mind on what it was about his colleague that he admired and liked, so that the urgency was taken out of his disapproval and before the day was up he wondered if he hadn't, after all, been a little harsh.

Nell spent the next few days full of her father: what he had said, the smartness of the flat, the West End address, the delicious sandwiches specially bought in, and the tasty slabs of cake. The taxi meter had already reached six pounds fifty by the time they got to Camden and then he was going all the way back into the West End. She speculated on the fat tip the driver would be given.

'How did it go, darling?'

'Oh, you know.'

'No problems, then?'

'Problems?'

'It went pretty well, then?'

'Think so.'

'And . . . um . . . did he seem . . . Did you think . . . Was it what you expected?'

'Yeah, you know.'

Nell could not wait for Wednesday to come round again. This time she prepared herself meticulously for her midweek date. She washed her hair on Tuesday after school because it was always at its best exactly twenty-four hours later. She shined her shoes, rubbing polish deep into the scuffs which she usually rather liked, buffing the leather with a yellow duster until it gleamed. She brushed down her blazer with her mother's clothes brush. Then she began thinking of things she might tell him. She was anxious that there shouldn't be looming gaps in the conversation, so she pieced together interesting stories and anecdotes of daring or morally taxing deeds, like the Smelly story, in which she was the heroine. All week she had talked about him constantly at school. 'My father goes everywhere in taxis,' she remarked to no one in particular. 'So fucking what!' a girl she barely knew replied.

After her first visit, when Fisher had felt she had turned her nose up, not impolitely, but noticeably (if the truth be told he had been rather impressed by this), at the fare he had provided (Didn't children like average, bland food? Wasn't that the thinking behind school dinners?) it was obvious that she had too high a regard for things of quality to be palmed off with pharmacy-bought sandwiches and this time he would lay on a more impressive spread. One of his patients was ill and, faced with a free hour, he had walked to Marylebone High Street and purchased the cream of what was on sale there.

'At my father's house there are generally three types of cake,' Nell told her friends at school. She had picked up his 'generally'. Often he began sentences with, 'I generally do', or 'I don't generally like'.

Fisher liked rule, rote, pattern, discipline and stability. His life was underwritten by a certain grammar, but it wasn't inflexible. He liked the idea of surprise and serendipity, but it was important for him that he had his footing at all times. Since childhood Fisher had taken an analytical approach to life that had extended to the habit of occasionally providing a mental running commentary on his own everyday actions as he went about them. 'He puts his knife and fork together on the plate, asks if he may leave the table, folds his napkin neatly, stands, tucks the chair in.' It was always in the third person, this neutral constant narrative in which he had observed himself as a child. If he had thought of consulting a psychologist about this kink in his personality ('The young man consults a doctor, delivers his story in long, sorry syllables'), or if his parents had done so when he was a child ('God forbid!' his father would have shouted), a psychologist might have told him it was a way of rooting himself very firmly in the present and absenting himself from it at one and the same time.

When the third Wednesday came Fisher had not had time to shop and he no longer trusted Mrs Summers to gauge his daughter's taste and so he and Nell walked to a café in the high street where he was well known. They made a huge fuss of Nell, bringing her, free, a biscuit in the shape of a ladybird covered with red icing and white chocolate dots. The two of them soon fell to discussing the other patrons of the café, wondering together about the various lives of these strangers: the woman in the cream trouser suit and bangles, the fat man eating cake and his tiny wife (Nell: 'I think she's tall enough to be a dwarf') eating salad. Fisher ordered tea for two and a macaroon which was backed with rice paper. 'And for the beautiful young lady?' the waiter enquired. He took Nell up to the shop window to choose a cake and together they picked out a coronet of little choux buns filled with cream and smothered in glossy chocolate sauce. It was brought to the table with a glass of milk. When her father saw the cake he raised his eyebrows. Nell could have kicked herself. She had been too greedy. Perhaps it was too expensive also. To make matters worse, when she bit into it the cake was disgusting. The cream was granular and cheesy, the chocolate was bitter and had been adulterated with coffee and seemed to taste of grit. Nell got it over and done with as quickly as possible. Her father looked up at the empty dish and asked her, smiling and excited, 'Will you have another? Go on, Nell, do,' and before she had a chance to think she had said 'Yes' and another sugary monstrosity was placed before her. Fisher made no effort to hide his delight at her appetite and the high spirits that went along with it. For himself he ordered another coffee.

Soon it was time to leave. Nell got up to go to the lavatory, where, to her surprise, she was promptly sick into the gleaming toilet bowl. The food had been far too rich for a little girl. 'Silly,' she said, dabbing at her mouth with some lavatory paper. She pulled the heavy metal chain three times before it would flush, all the while looking in the opposite direction: the sight as well as the acrid smell of the chewed-up pieces of brown and orange food swimming in bile and glistening with saliva would have made her vomit again. Outside the cubicle she washed her face, combed her hair and went to meet her father. She felt better without the revolting cakes inside her. He hailed a taxi and climbed in after her. 'To Camden please and then to Grosvenor Square,' he said. As the taxi drew into her road Fisher asked her if she wanted some pocket money. 'OK,' Nell said. 'What would you like?' her father asked her. '80p?' she suggested after some thought. He counted out the coins. 'That's extremely modest,' he told her mildly. 'Oh, good,' Nell said. She'd got something right at last.

The next evening Nell decided to write a letter to her father. If she sent it off in the morning they would be together in some ways at the weekend, thus tiding them over until the following Wednesday.

Dear Richard,
I hope you are very well. I am making a trifle as there's talk of Laura and her mother coming over for supper. We have little sponge cakes and fruit and I'm making some custard as I write this letter which is not terribly sensible. It'll have cream and

toasted, slivered almonds on the top.

Yesterday at school we did sonnets. Mine only had thirteen lines and Mrs Moorland ticked me off about it and suggested an extra line which didn't work at all. Luckily I managed to persuade her I was right. It's absolutely not good at all, but I quite like it. See you Wed.,

> *Love from Nell*

PS I wish I saw more of you

Nell rewrote the letter on a postcard, omitting the last line, and sent it off.

On Wednesday, Fisher thanked her for the card. 'I didn't reply,' he said, 'because I knew I'd be seeing you.'

'Oh, you weren't meant to. That wasn't what I meant at all.'

She wrote to him again after their next meeting.

Dear Richard,

Thanks for a lovely tea today. That blackcurrant jam certainly was delicious although I think I had too much. I went round to Laura's this evening. Laura's mother seems to have struck up a romance with one of the men in the office who wears grey shoes and says, 'See you as and when', and 'There's someone on the blower.' Laura is trying to be 'philosophical' about it.

I hope you are keeping warm now that the cold weather has set in.

> *See you V.S.*
> *Love Nell.*

Chapter 3

Vastly impressed by the smartness of his address, the gleaming orderliness of his affairs and the relaxed dignity which seemed to govern all his actions, in no time at all it seemed to Nell that Richard Fisher was quite the most remarkable person she had ever met. Even the very peripheral aspects of him, areas in which it would have been quite permissible for a hero not to shine, benefited from the same thorough, high-class consideration. His socks, for instance, when she looked at them carefully, did have something particularly nice about them. One day she gathered up courage to say so and he told her they were from Brooks Brothers in New York and he liked them because they didn't have elastic at the tops (which irritated the skin), and had to be kept up with willpower which he was glad to have the opportunity to exercise. American cotton, he said, was often softer than other kinds of cotton and when, in September, Nell couldn't help noticing that the fabric of his socks looked thicker, he said he had gone on to heavier, winter-weight fabric which was half merino wool and half cashmere. Nell was dying to ask how much each pair cost – it might have been as much as thirty pounds, she speculated – but she held her tongue, guessing (correctly) that this sort of enquiry might annoy him. The weekly meetings continued as regular as clockwork, and after five months Nell was living for Wednesdays.

Sometimes her father read poetry to her, and occasionally short stories from the *New Yorker*. Fisher's manner of reading was so animated and commanding that although he read her works by a variety of quite different writers, in her mind all the various styles could not compete with his startlingly clear voice and merged into the works of a single persona, immediately recognizable by her father's fine instincts and acute perceptions. (Later on it occurred to her that a shopping list would have resonated with his superior personality traits had he read it aloud to her, but the aspects of their lives that featured such ordinary activities they did not share.) Nell listened to his reading and it seemed to her that there was one writer who could turn his hand to tender short stories, robust and humorous mediaeval poems, several poignant love lyrics, cautionary tales, high tragic speeches and witty, knowing observations about New York City.

Generally they went out now on Wednesdays, often to a nearby hotel which served unwieldy set teas on three-tiered scalloped cake stands. On other occasions they went back to the café on the high street where the waiter continued to fuss over Nell, bringing her little treats and compliments, while her father talked to her about books. To Fisher his profession and his love of reading stemmed from the same side of him, the part that was fascinated by words and stories. Being with her father in this respect was an education for Nell. His plan for her to attend his old school having been thwarted by her mother's desire to keep Nell at home and not miles away at some boarding school, Fisher was glad to be able to contribute to her knowledge in this way, to introduce her, fresh, alert and vastly susceptible as she was, to all the things he liked. In her twelfth year they read and discussed all the Jane Austens, most of the poetry in the *Oxford Book of English Verse*, Shakespeare's comedies, some Conrad, some Scott, *The Rape of the Lock* and *Aunts Aren't Gentlemen* by P. G. Wodehouse. At the end of the summer term Nell was able to inform her father that she had won a scholarship to the local girls' high school.

In a year, meeting once a week, Nell and Fisher had become as thick as thieves. For her twelfth birthday he took her to a bookshop he liked and bought her fine editions of all the major English poets. For his fiftieth birthday Nell cut out pictures of various models, actresses and film stars in evening clothes and pasted them into a scrapbook. Underneath the random images of perfect womanhood, or near perfect as some of them had a bit of elbow or shin lopped off through hasty scissor work, Nell copied out the words to 'My Heart Belongs to Daddy' in her best handwriting, wrapped the parcel in white tissue, red ribbon and a pink rose and left it on her father's doorstep on the right day. She called him Daddy now. It had been 'that man' at first, and then 'Richard' and then 'Dad', the first time tentatively, her eyes on him for any sign that he might mind. From Dad to Daddy had been a short step when once she had had to call him from a small distance, 'Daddeeeee' being easier on the vocal chords than 'Daaaaad'.

Fisher liked the gift well enough.

If Nell had a clear idea of what she liked about Fisher – the sheer length of him, the beautiful clothes, his being right all the time – she was also beginning to build up a picture of what *he* liked in a person. Passing an enormous turkey, the centrepiece in a butcher's shop Christmas display, Nell had said, 'Look, the Loch Ness Turkey', and he had smiled at her approvingly. 'When I was seven, I quite wanted to be a nun,' Nell said on a separate occasion, 'because I thought it would be completely extreme', and Fisher looked up, his eyes alert, interested. 'Have you read Carlyle's *On Heroes and Hero Worship*?' she asked him, having noticed the title on the school library's shelves.

'No, I haven't,' Fisher said. 'Is it any good?'

'I'm not sure,' Nell answered, 'but I think the title's completely good.'

'I quite agree.' Fisher inclined his head towards her.

Once, when Nell was walking along a street with him, looking for a tea shop, jogging every few steps to keep up with his great strides, she had swiftly darted round to say something she suddenly thought might interest him, and turned back only to crash her

45

forehead and her left leg into a lamppost. Of course she had made out that it hadn't hurt at all, but all the evidence stood against her. There was an enormous purple lump on her brow and a graze on her knee which dripped blood down her shin. Yet when he asked if they shouldn't turn back, if she wasn't in rather a lot of pain, she just answered, as he sometimes did, 'God, no!' 'Brave girl,' he said quietly into the air. (Despite all his training first in medicine, then psychiatry, psychology and psychoanalytic psychotherapy, Fisher still believed, in his heart of hearts, that it was rather heroic not to show one's feelings.)

The things that Fisher didn't like also became clear over time and Nell avoided them as best she could. The use of inexact language needled him.

'Laura's mother has an on-going love affair with one of the men at the office.'

'I've never heard the word on-going spoken before, I've just seen it written in the newspaper. I don't expect it means anything much. Do you?'

Nell was too crushed to explain. On-going certainly wasn't a phrase she had used before, but she hadn't used it lightly, and it did seem particularly applicable in this instance. The romance in question had been going on every Thursday afternoon for the last eighteen months and Laura and her brother and Nell all referred to it as Happy Thursday.

Another time she had been taken by her mother to an exhibition of paintings, part of an art school graduation show, which she had described afterwards to her father.

She had liked the work, she told her father, and added that all the paintings had been hugely big. A few days later he had brought it up again. 'I don't understand. You surely didn't think they were good *because* they were big.'

'That isn't what I said,' Nell replied, close to tears.

Nell knew that Fisher liked it when she said unusual, mildly surprising things, but had an idea that there was a certain line that shouldn't be crossed. When she pictured the toddler lying on the floor kicking its legs and banging its heels, its dress all ridden up, its nappy coming off, Nell winced.

'Did you have a good tea, darling?' Mrs Dorney asked her daughter on the doorstep.

Nell, having wrenched herself from the warmth and safety of the taxi cab, was often sharp at these moments. 'Very nice, thank you,' she replied curtly. But she avoided her mother's curious gaze and kept her eyes on the taxi disappearing down the street until it was no bigger than a dot.

'Is Dad well?'

'Extremely well.' Nell smiled. 'Yeah, we had tea at Brown's Hotel.'

'Oh, did you? He used to take me there when I first knew him. It's rather nice, isn't it? I remember they used to have enormous cakes filled with jam and cream and then they'd bring you a dish of jam and a bowl of cream as well to go with them. It always used to make me laugh and then one time, the old waiter who used to be kind to us, he's probably still there actually, he—'

47

'I think I might go and have a bath,' Nell said and left the room to fetch a clean towel from the airing cupboard.

An hour later there was a knock on Nell's bedroom door. Nell was sitting on her bed painting her toenails. 'Hello, yes?' she called out.

Her mother put her head round the door. 'Nell, darling, I don't want you to take this the wrong way or anything . . . '

'Here we go,' Nell said silently under her breath.

' . . . But the thing is I'm a bit worried about you.'

'Oh?'

'About you and Dad.'

'Oh?'

'Well, you will be careful, won't you?'

'What d'you mean, careful?'

'I think what I'm trying to say is, it's really wonderful to me that you seem to be getting on so well, but I—'

'What?'

'I'm just worried. I don't want you to be disappointed. He's very good at making one feel special, and, I suppose I'm worried that he might let you down somehow. That it might all end in tears.'

'Jealous,' Nell thought.

'I know it's not at all the same, but I suppose that I feel in a way I just don't want you to have to go through what I went through, with him I mean. Everything being so wonderful and then so awful.'

'We aren't exactly thinking of getting married, you know.'

'I know that, Nell. I just don't want you getting your heart broken, that's all. I'm just warning you. I know he's terribly handsome and glamorous and all the rest of it, but he's pretty selfish in a lot of ways, and I think you should hold yourself back a bit, just in case.'

'Okey doke,' Nell said absently. She was applying another coat of nail varnish to her toes. Her mother left the room, closing the door quietly. 'Stupid cow,' Nell said, waving her hand to and fro across her feet to make the polish dry more quickly. 'You stupid cow,' she said, and gave her head three sharp little raps with her fist.

The next morning when Nell came down to breakfast she noticed her mother looking at her with a particular intensity. 'I think it's about time we got you a bra, Nell.'

'Is this anything to do with last night?'

'Of course not. Laura's mother and I were talking about it the other day.'

'What! Talking about my ti—'

'No, silly, that you and Laura were both, how did she put it, "turning into young women" or something. Anyway, so then we thought maybe we could all go shopping together.'

'Yeah, whatever,' Nell said, but alone in her room she felt crushed. 'I mean, why don't you flaming sell tickets?'

That Saturday, Nell and Laura went to buy their first bras together, Laura having refused point blank the benefit of the mothers' experience and her mother eventually agreeing to the trip once she had phoned up Dickins and Jones and spoken to their Mrs Brackett, who assured her that the young ladies would be in good hands. Mrs Nesbitt telephoned Nell's mother. 'I told the girls there was a measuring service. You should have seen their faces! I said, I don't care, you can grimace as much as you like, you'll be thanking me in the end. It can make a world of difference being fitted properly. You don't want to come away with anything sloppy, I said. End up all drooped and sagging. Then both of them couldn't stop laughing. I do hope they'll be all right.'

Nell and Laura took the escalator to the third floor, making a brief stop to browse at the make-up counter, where Nell was asked, 'Do you suffer from high colour in winter?' so quickly that she thought she was being addressed in a strange language.

In the lingerie department, Laura and Nell suffered the indignity of bust measurement by Mrs Brackett. 'It's essential to get the size exactly right, darling,' Laura imitated her mother's clipped tones. After they had been measured: 'Your first, is it dear? I think your mother telephoned the store.' (Blushes.) The senior assistant led them to the 'My First Bra' teen bra carousel and left them there to choose, but the girls soon drifted towards the more exotic lines. Nell and Laura fingered the vast array of different designs on the third floor. Black and lacy, sporty stretch cotton-Lycra, French checked models with high-cut briefs to match, underwired, uplift, padded, scalloped, silk-satin, frilly, half-cup, full-cup, nautical stripes, red polka dots, mauve lace . . .

'What d'you think?' Nell held up a huge, stretch-lace, black plunging number against herself. 'It's a 40DD. Will it suit me?'

'Might be a tight fit,' Laura said, squashing the two hollow netted skull-sized cups together.

'So, d'you think we should go for onwards and upwards or inwards and chinwards?' Nell asked.

'I don't know,' Laura said. 'Onwards and upwards *is* our school motto.'

'We certainly should take that into account.'

'But should a brassière lift and separate or roll together? We should be told.'

The assistant reappeared. 'Many women favour a variety of garments so that a number of different looks can be achieved.'

'I see,' Nell said politely.

After a while Nell and Laura got bored. 'We're going to go and have a think,' Nell told the assistant and they left the shop.

'I couldn't help noticing that they were all very expensive,' Laura said.

'I know. Maybe we should have a look in Marks and Sparks. What size were we again?'

'32B,' Laura reminded her.

They walked down Oxford Street until they reached the new flagship store at Marble Arch where they each bought the same two bras, one black and one white from the Teen Dream range. Each garment was made from cotton and was completely plain apart from a small ribbon bow where the cups joined. 'Very suitable,' Nell said.

'Anyway, we'll grow out of them soon with any luck,' Laura laughed.

After their shopping they wandered into a nearby burger bar and ordered two coffees and an apple pie to share. When they had finished the hot sweet pie Nell licked her lips, took a packet of ten Silk Cut ultra-mild out of her pocket.

'What d'you think?' she said to Laura.

'I'm not sure.'

'I feel we ought to somehow, now we're . . . ' she shook their green carrier bags, 'women and all.'

'Well look, why don't we have one each and then throw the packet away?'

'OK. But no coughing, all right?' Nell ordered.

'All right.'

Nell lit her cigarette and lit one for Laura. She took a puff. The taste of apple pie was still in her mouth and the hot sweetness and cinnamon went well with the cigarette's flavour. 'It's lovely, ' she said. But Laura was coughing all over the place.

'You all right?' Nell said, posing her cigarette on the edge of the foil ashtray.

'Fine. I just don't like it, that's all. I'm not one of nature's smokers.'

'God, I am. I think I'm hooked already!'

'Oh yeah.'

Nell took a few more tentative puffs. 'Dee-licious,' she said.

'So have you seen your dad lately,' Laura asked.

'I'm seeing him on Wednesday, actually.'

'You gonna tell him about today?'

'What, smoking, you mean?'

'No, tits,' she said, tweaking Nell's left nipple.

'I don't think so somehow. I tell you what, though. He only lives about ten minutes from here. I could show you his house if you like.'

'Yeah?'

'Yeah, let's go,' and the two girls got up, leaving the packet of cigarettes amateurishly on the table, much to the delight of their neighbour.

They walked the brisk half-mile to Wimpole Street.

'That's the house, over there,' said Nell pointing.

'Shall we go and say Hello?'

'I don't know. It might not be a good time. What do you think?'

'It's up to you, I don't mind. Hey, Nell, look at that woman over there.'

'Where?'

'Over there, by the corner, walking this way now.'

'Oh yeah. Wow.'

'Isn't she beautiful?'

'Very. Oh my God, she's going into my dad's house. That's my dad's house. Look she's going up to number seventy-two.'

'She's pressed the bell.'

'The bottom one?'

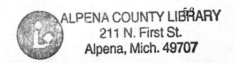

'I can't see. Oh yeah, now there's a man answering the door. He's really tall and he's wearing a dark suit.'

'It's my dad,' Nell said. 'We'd better disappear.'

'Maybe we should wait.'

'What for?'

'Maybe she won't be long.'

'D'you want to ring the bell and find out what's going on? It's probably just an old friend or something.'

'I doubt it somehow.'

'Well, it might be.'

'She was all tarted up and everything.'

'True, but it is Saturday. She'd probably been round the shops. People do get done up to go shopping sometimes so that the shop assistants treat them with respect.'

'Maybe I should telephone.'

'What would you say?'

'I don't know, see if she picked up the phone or something.'

'You could. There's a phone box over there.'

They both squeezed into the booth and Nell dialled the number.'

'Hello.' It was a woman's voice.

'Oh hullo. Um, hello, yes.'

'Is that you, Nell?'

'Oh, Mrs Summers.'

'Hello dear, how are you?'

'Fine.'

'I'm afraid your father's with someone at the

moment but he'll be free at ten to four. Shall I get him to ring you then?'

'I'm in a call box.'

'Oh, I see. Well perhaps you'd like to ring back in about an hour. Or would you like me to pass on a message?'

'Would you not tell him I called.'

'Not tell him?'

'That's right, not mention it.'

'All right then, dear.'

'Thank you very much.'

'Not at all, dear. Goodbye.'

Fisher telephoned the house that evening. It was something he never did: they had their Wednesday arrangement; there was an understanding that it was a permanent fixture and so there was no need for him to make other contact. When she heard the voice at the other end of the line, formal but warm, Nell assumed that Mrs Summers had said something, but if this was the case her father did not let on.

'I thought, for a change, we might have some dinner, out somewhere, on Wednesday, if you'd like. Perhaps you could meet me at seven and we could have a drink at me and then go on. Would that suit?'

'Be lovely,' Nell said.

'Very good. I'll see you then. Bye.'

Nell had never been to a restaurant with her father before. There had been numerous cafés and hotel tea rooms, but never anywhere one might find a candle on the table or a bottle of wine. At the prospect of their dinner together, Nell felt happy in the extreme. Some-how, she had accrued more status with him, been promoted from high tea to a proper adult meal, from girl to woman. Nell laughed. Could it be connected to the pair of 32Bs? Nell knew she looked older than her thirteen years. Three times, recently, her status as a child had been called into question. Once at the cinema where the usher had asked for proof that she was under sixteen (ask me O-Level maths, she thought of saying, I won't know it); once on the bus where the bus conductor had only grudgingly charged her a half fare and once by a boy in the bus queue who had assumed she was in the fifth year at school.

Nell arrived twenty minutes early at Bond Street station, where she had arranged to meet Fisher. There was a man outside the entrance selling early daffodils and Nell bought a large bunch, which he wrapped in white paper printed with bright red roses and green leaves. Nell's father arrived early also and started reading his paper without even looking out for her and Nell held herself out of his view until it was a few minutes to seven. Then she called hello in his direction. She gave him the flowers. 'How lovely to see you.' They kissed hello and walked up Oxford Street. Fisher wore a heavy blue coat over his dark suit. As they turned into Bond Street he said, 'If you're cold, do say and we'll jump into a taxi.'

'I'm completely fine,' Nell said.

Her father suddenly let out a huge yawn.

'Tired?'

'Long day, I'm afraid. I'm working very hard at the moment, tying up a lot of loose ends.'

'At Wimpole Street?'

'That's right.'

'What exactly do you do at Wimpole Street, Dad?'

'Well, people come to see me, generally three or four times a week and Mrs Summers lets them in and we talk for fifty minutes and sometimes I prescribe them medicine, but mainly they tell me what's on their mind and I make an interpretation of what has or hasn't been said according to what my training has taught me, and my medical experience and also my instincts, and then we discuss the interpretation.'

'And does it happen at weekends?'

'I do see two patients on Saturday afternoon, yes.'

'Is one of them a smart lady in a fur coat? It's just I saw her going into your house when I was passing.'

'Your description does fit a certain patient of mine.'

'And what's wrong with her?'

'Ah – that I can't tell you. It would be quite wrong of me to discuss my patients with another party.'

They were walking down Grosvenor Street by this time and Fisher took Nell's arm and turned them both into a doorway, just before they reached the Square. He drew a bunch of keys from an inside pocket and unlocked the door.

'Where are we going?'

'This is where I live.' They were climbing the stairs. Fisher took them two at a time and Nell trotted along behind him. 'I thought it might amuse you to see it.'

'But you live at Wimpole.'

'No, that's just where I see my patients.'

'You don't sleep there?'

'No. This is where I live,' he repeated.

'But I thought of you at night sitting in the drawing room at Wimpole, with those packets of cake like when I first came to see you.'

'You mean the waiting room,' he laughed.

The waiting room! Only the waiting room.

'I just thought it would be easier for us to meet there and your mother thought so, it being that bit nearer school and so on.'

'Oh, I see,' Nell said.

Nearly there, Fisher told her, and though Nell could see there was only one more flight of stairs to be climbed, she stopped for a moment to catch her breath. There were tears in her eyes. They had drunk tea together in a waiting room, like strangers in a railway station or a hospital. The high spirits of the afternoon had dwindled to nothing. She took a deep breath and took the last set of stairs and entered her father's flat. The place seemed ruined for her now: dark and oppressive with its brown velvet furniture, wine-coloured curtains, dark rugs, dark shiny bookcases and dark leather-topped desk spilling heavy cream envelopes, sheets of type, open books scored with pencil and a large pile of newspaper clippings.

Nell took the small armchair that was offered to her and folded her arms while Fisher paced about the room, putting stray papers into piles, straightening chairs, closing books, opening and closing drawers. He filled a glass jar with water for her flowers. Nell fixed her eyes firmly to the ground. After a few more minutes of near-silent arrangings, Fisher said, 'Let's go to the restaurant.' They decided to walk to the restaurant, which was behind Grosvenor Square. Fisher asked Nell what she'd like, but all she could manage to say, in a small and shaky voice, was that she'd have what he was having. The waiters brought them oysters and Fisher ate all his and then all hers. Next came two small whole lobsters. Fisher said, 'It's often better to have a very small whole one than half a large one.'

'Is that true of other things like avocados?' Nell asked, but Fisher didn't answer. He was trying to attract the attention of the wine waiter and anyway it might have been a stupid thing to say. Nell prized the lobster flesh out of its shell and began to eat.

'How is it?' Fisher enquired.

'Completely delicious.'

'Thank goodness for that,' Fisher said. Then, encouraged, he put down his fork. 'I'm sorry if you felt misled about the room, Nell. It hadn't occurred to me that you might have thought it was my house. It was foolish of me not to have taken it into account. I'm very sorry, Nell. Can you let it go?'

'I think I might just get over it in time,' Nell replied coyly.

'Thanks.' Fisher smiled at his daughter.

Nell suddenly felt buoyant and festive, digging her fork deep into the crevices of the lobster and feeling its thin juices wet and itchy on her hands. 'Guess what happened at the weekend? I was in Boots in Oxford Street and an Arab man came up to me and he said, "Miss, could I ask you something please?" So I said, "What?" And he said, "I know that when women wash their hands they sometimes like to put a cream on afterwards. I have no idea about it – do you think you could advise me as to which would be good creams to buy?" So I picked out one, this French make, *Jeunesse des Mains*, that Laura's mother uses, and he thanked me and I carried on with my shopping, but then the next thing I know, he is standing right behind me saying, "Perhaps you would allow me to buy you one also." "No thank you," I said. "I'm really quite fine." "Ah," he said, "perhaps you no like this cream, perhaps there's something else." "Honestly," I said, "there's really nothing I want." And then he took a basket from the stack and started filling it with all this stuff: hair spray, deodorant, air freshener, lipstick, shampoo, none of which I wanted in the least. "I want to buy this for you," he said. "I insist. You have been so kind." He just wouldn't take no for an answer so in the end I picked up a large tube of toothpaste and said, "Look, if you really want to get me something you can get me this." Which he did. Anyway, so I left the shop and he's running after me saying, "Can I invite you for coffee?" "I'm in a bit of a hurry," I said. "It's late-night shopping Thursday, can I take you shopping? Meet me in the lobby of the Selfridge Hotel at six p.m. I invite you. I invite you." "No thank you," I said. "I just want to thank you properly," he called after me. At this point people were looking at us, so I just said, "Goodbye, thanks for the toothpaste," and ran, and he didn't follow but I heard him shouting, "Six o'clock, the Selfridge Hotel. In the lobby. Six o'clock. We go shopping. I invite you." '

'And will you go to the Hotel?' Fisher asked.

'I thought I wouldn't.'

'Very sensible,' Fisher replied.

Nell had ordered a great pudding of several different types of ice-cream with fruit and biscuits and nuts and sauce. To accompany it a waiter brought a small silver bucket filled with cream and a silver ladle and suggested that Nell help herself, which she did. Her father's hand held a small black coffee.

Nell took a mouthful of her pudding. 'Complete Heaven,' she said.

'Good.' Fisher took a deep breath. 'Look, Nell, you've probably guessed that I've brought you here because there's something I want to tell you.'

This had not occurred to Nell. She could tell from his voice that it must be something bad and she braced her leg hard against the leg of the table and pressed her back into the back of the chair while she waited for his news. 'Oh yes?' she said casually.

'The thing is, I've got to go to America.'

'Holiday?' Nell asked.

'No, Nell. I've been offered a job. In fact it's an academic post, but it's what I've been hoping for. It would allow me to practise, teach and carry on with my own research. It's just too good an opportunity to turn down. Initially it's a three-year contract, but with any luck I'll be able to extend it. I hope you'll come out in the holidays, as often as you like. I'll have a house there and probably a pool and . . . '

Nell switched off and concentrated on finishing her dessert. Icy spoonful followed icy spoonful. The front of her head ached sharply from the cold but she carried on . . . 'Of course we'll write often . . . ' Nell surveyed the restaurant's decor. It was old-fashioned in a comfortable, masculine sort of way; the room was long and narrow like a dining car on a very grand train.

'Unfortunately, I have to go almost straight away, because the man I'm replacing died suddenly . . . '

There were several layers of thick white cloths on the tables and gleaming silver and dark green velvet curtains blocking out the light from the street. Nell realized her father had stopped talking and was now looking at her. Nell spooned up the last drops of cream. 'Will you excuse me for a moment?' she said.

She took small quick steps to the ladies', where she was sick all over the floor. The sick was thick and smooth and pale, like melted ice-cream, but studded with occasional pieces of garish glacé cherry. Nell tore off several sheets of lavatory paper, tucked her skirt into her pants and knelt down on the floor to clear away the mess. The operation took some time; when she had finally removed all traces of the liquid and wiped her face and shoes and returned to the table, her father had paid the bill. She thanked him for the meal and they confirmed their last tea, which would be on the following Wednesday, usual time. But when Wednesday came round Nell was unwell. She had a slight temperature and felt tired and achy and her mother judged it best that she should spend the day in bed. Fisher phoned to say his goodbyes, but Nell was sleeping.

'Could you not wake her?' he asked her mother.

'Of all the fucking cruel things you've done, Richard,' Mrs Dorney spat out at him through clenched teeth, 'this has to be about the very lowest.' And before he had a chance to retort she had replaced the receiver.

Chapter 4

Nell met Bill Marnie for the first time, if you could call it a meeting, when she was fifteen. He was doing a reading from his new collection of poems at a bookshop in Charing Cross Road and she was in the audience with Laura. They had come straight from school and wore blue and white gingham dresses that had Peter Pan collars edged with blue piping – the summer uniform of Chesterfield High. Each girl had a navy blue jumper tied round her middle and a blue nylon sack of books slung over one shoulder.

They settled into the wooden seats that the staff of the bookshop had arranged in neat rows. The manager of the shop gave a brief speech about the importance of supporting poetry. There was a restrained burst of applause. Then the room fell silent. Bill Marnie walked onto the short impromptu platform in the crowded bookshop in his light grey suit and crumpled white shirt and sat down in a chair like theirs. From his jacket pocket he drew a thin book thickened by strips of paper and began leafing through the pages. He took a sip from his glass of red wine and looked up for a moment at the audience. 'Evening,' he said, his voice exactly caught between nervousness and irony. A gentle murmur of laughter and 'Good Evening' came back from the rows of people, largely women, who had come to hear the performance. At the sound of his voice, Laura gave Nell a great dig in the ribs and mouthed the words, 'Oh my God.' At this Nell got the giggles. She put her hand across her mouth, but she was laughing so much that her whole head shook. An elderly lady sitting next to them raised her eyebrows, an old man in front of them dealt the girls an indulgent smile. Marnie himself, looking stern and eminent and a little lost gave a small, dry cough and the show began.

Laura had had a thing about Bill Marnie ever since she had seen a picture of him in one of the Sunday supplements. She liked his nose, the angle of which she found intelligent. She admired the sweep of his hair and what she termed his lean, curious look. She also praised his poetry. It was resonant and remote and he made his words count, she said. She showed the picture to Nell. 'Guess how old?' she asked.

'Twenty-eight. No, thirty-four,' Nell said.

'Forty-one.'

'No!'

'Yep, forty-one, three months and five days.'

Marnie's poetry had one main theme: missingness. He called it his English preoccupation. Absences, in poetry, in life, commanded the same sort of meticulous attention from him as presences. Marnie's was a late-

Romantic poetry, full of lost Edens, near misses, forlorn strivings, a preoccupation with the gap between how things were and what there was room to hope for. His latest collection, *Evening Poems*, had been described in one of the Sunday papers which had run a feature on Marnie (including a photograph of him sitting at his desk amid a sea of papers with a tumbler of whisky in one hand and a red-and-black striped pencil in the other), as a matrix of longing.

Laura said Marnie's poetic forms were neat and highly wrought to contain the sprawl of emotions within. This struck Nell as sensible. After all, wasn't this the reason you brushed your hair every morning? He was very attractive to look at, short dark hair with the hint of a curl to it, deep, faintly severe grey eyes, a huge thin-lipped smile, long straight nose. No one to iron his shirt though, each of the girls thought, unless it was an affectation, a deliberate oversight to make him look more poetical. After he had read his last poem, a villanelle entitled 'Oh Dear What Can the Matter Be?', Laura dug her in the ribs again. 'I'm in love,' she whispered.

'I quite agree,' said Nell. 'I quite agree.'

A question-and-answer session followed the reading. 'Can you tell us a little bit about how you came to be a poet. Had you always wanted to be one?' asked a skinny, ardent-sounding woman, who was buttoned tightly into a navy coat.

Marnie cleared his throat. 'When I was young I was dying to do something good. I used to read all day long and at night; I suppose insomnia made me more learned. All my waking time when I wasn't reading I used to daydream about writing something really important, something that would enable me to satisfy certain great questions. You can see I was very full of myself.'

The audience nodded and smiled as one.

'I used to think about Coleridge seeking a subject for a poem that would give him "equal room for description, incident, and impassioned reflections on men, nature and society, yet supply in itself a natural connection to the parts and unity to the whole". But, not very surprisingly I just couldn't put my finger on anything.' He paused. 'Of course, to try and start with a long poem was a crazy idea.'

'I don't know,' Nell said to Laura, shrugging her shoulders.

'So then I searched for two years for the perfect subject. I was about seventeen at this point. I thought that if I concentrated my brain, flexed it hard up against what I was reading, then the sheer force of the scrutiny would force some life into what I was writing. You see, I'd heard that poetry came out of poetry. I suppose my mistake was trying too hard. To make matters worse, the other people I knew who were writing poems then, just people I met at university, all seemed to have backgrounds that deeply affected their attitude to language. One had lived in Russia for three years, another had stammered very badly in his adolescent years, another had grown up in a house where Welsh was spoken as well as English, and so on. I remember feeling cheated that I had not experienced anything of this nature that might distinguish my grasp of English. Then I grew depressed that all the best subjects had been taken, the myths and legends, the great Christian themes, even the forms, sonnets, quatrains, couplets, villanelles – it all seemed pretty hopeless somehow.'

Marnie stopped briefly and pulled an odd face which indicated exasperation with his silly adolescent self, but it was affectionately done, indulgent, in the way that one might indulge a child.

'Then one day I read a review of a poet I admired which said the poet had taken the subject of the self and treated it with the same kind of awe and formality that the pre-Romantic poets would have used writing about a grand theme such as the Fall of Man or The Progress of the Soul. I read Blackmur's comment that poetry "not only expresses the matter in hand but adds to the stock of available reality". I fell in love. I fell out of love. I was seriously ill for a while, then I recovered. I started writing things that focused on my quarrels with myself. I realized that subject matter was not as important as I had once thought it. At last there seemed to be a point to the ups and downs of my inner life. It seemed that with the proper treatment they might open out into something more, a larger realm of banalities and heroics than merely the personal.'

Marnie stopped talking. No one else had a question. The manager of the bookshop thanked Marnie and indicated a corner of the shop where *Evening Poems* could be purchased. The audience clapped and that was it.

Nell knew there was a pub adjacent to the bookshop. Chances were he would be heading that way. It was well known that Bill Marnie liked a drink. Both girls were accustomed to drinking in pubs, but the school uniforms presented an obstacle. They decided to put on their jumpers and hide their schoolgirl collars underneath the woolly necklines. Two girls in blue jumpers and matching checked skirts . . . well it wouldn't fool many people but it was better than before. Several members of the audience had purchased a copy of *Evening Poems* and were waiting for Marnie to sign the fly leaf in the hope that next to his simple signature he might impart some tender good wishes.

'We are the youngest and most alluring women here,' Nell said, unravelling her glossy dark hair from its schoolgirl plait and shaking the kinky locks free.

'Not difficult,' Laura replied.

(Neither of the girls bought Marnie's book. If they clubbed together their money they were still 50p short of the cover price.) Marnie was slowly edging his way towards them.

'Ask him to come for a drink,' Laura hissed. 'Quick.'

Marnie was standing about fourteen inches from Nell. She could smell him. Toothpaste and cigarette smoke. Perfect.

'Really enjoyed it,' Nell said.

He looked up, cool, aloof, very slightly intimate.

'Y'didn't think it was a bit bland?'

'OH, NO,' Nell said. 'We didn't think it was bland at all. In fact everyone seemed to . . . to enjoy it very much.' She realized her legs were trembling. Marnie was nodding heavily, but his heart wasn't really in it, certainly wasn't in his mouth as Nell's was. Nell and Laura were standing in front of him, and in front of the girls there was another small group of middle-aged, pinched, academic-looking women. Marnie had quite a following among such types. Nell could not move until the women moved and he could not move until she did. 'S'like Piccadilly Circus,' Laura said. Marnie coughed. We are getting on his nerves as well as in his way, Nell thought. It was now or never. Aware that their choice of words had been poor and flat so far, Nell searched for a canny idiom in which to continue the conversation. 'Um, could we . . . we'd very much like to . . . to . . . to . . . dish you a drink,' she said, hitting the nail, she felt, squarely on the thumb.

'I was just going to the gents',' Marnie said, and Nell felt he was intimating, 'How can you speak of banal social matters when important human functions are at stake?' But then kindly, after that, he added, 'I'll be in the pub next door. So if . . . ' He stopped talking and went off to the gents', leaving Nell and Laura to make their way into the pub.

'He's so handsome,' said Laura, as the two of them chose a faded red velvet booth in the small, dimly lit room, just a few feet from the bar, so that Nell had a good view of the pub door and Laura could see who was buying drinks. 'Talk about multiple orgasms!'

'I think I'm going to have to marry him,' Nell whispered into Laura's ear and when she leaned back into her seat again, to her horror Marnie was passing right behind her, smiling, always smiling. Her face went crimson and for some reason, on seeing him, Nell stood up, immediately lost her footing and suddenly she was sitting down almost on top of Laura. Marnie kindly looked away. 'Do you think he heard?' Nell was shaking. They were sitting side by side now.

'I wouldn't have thought so,' Laura reassured her.

They looked up. Marnie was standing at the bar now, vaguely trying to attract the attention of the barmaid.

'It's a bit rough to offer him a drink and then to forget about it completely,' said Nell. Marnie was still at the bar with no drink, ignored as newcomers to the bar bought their drinks before him. Nell got up.

'I hope they'll serve you,' Laura said, tucking Nell's school collar inside her jumper again.

She sidled casually up to the bar, stomach pulled in, head tossed back, trying to look eighteen. 'How about that drink?' she asked him gently.

'I'm with a few people. I can't really land you with a whole round,' said Marnie.

Nell tried again. 'I know, why don't you get theirs and I'll get yours?' But when she looked up at his face it seemed to be saying that this arrangement was quite untenable. Nell, crushed, ordered a vodka and orange for her and Laura to share and went back to the booth. She lit a cigarette. Marnie was talking to a TV arts programme presenter whom she recognized. They'd lost him now. The two girls sat, deflated, taking turns at sipping and puffing.

'Would you mind if I cadged a cigarette off you?' Marnie had suddenly appeared again.

'That'll do!' Nell said, triumphant, and gave him four, but Marnie didn't laugh and simply said, 'Just one, thanks.' She blushed again. As she was holding a box of matches in her hand anyway she struck one for him and was about to bend forward to light his cigarette when she was paralysed by the intimacy of the gesture; it seemed too embarrassing. His cigarette was already between his lips. To light it would be a direct communciation between her fingers and his mouth. Marnie waited. She could see him waiting, so she had to go through with it. The cigarette caught the fire from the match immediately. Marnie leaned away. 'So,' he said, blowing a couple of smoke rings in the opposite direction, 'do you two write poetry?' What a question! Laura opened her mouth and closed it and Nell said vaguely, after a few moments, 'Well, we're . . . we're feeling around a bit.' Marnie looked mildly amused at this. We are woeful amateurs, thought Nell. She tried a different tack. 'We're great fans of Berryman. He's our real cup of tea.' Nell winced at her own words. I'm speaking English like a first-year language student she thought.

'No, really? Brian Merryman? How extraordinary!'

'Not Brian Merryman, John Berryman,' Nell said.

'Oh,' Marnie answered. They had disappointed him, perhaps.

'So,' he tried once more, 'have you been to any other events in this series?' Nell had been to a talk on an American poet in a church hall in Piccadilly, all about worms, but exhausted by the tenseness of the conversation, the name went straight out of her head and she collapsed into giggles. They were waiting. Laura said his face had been all concern and bewilderment. Finally Nell said, 'Oh, yes, went to a talk on Wallace Stevens.' Marnie nodded. They were all relieved that she had found her voice. That was it. Marnie went off to join his friends. The absolute best he could have thought, Nell said despairingly to Laura's shoulder was, 'What very funny girls.'

Weary and crestfallen, the two schoolgirls finished their drinks and got up to go. But as they made their way to the door to their horror they saw that Marnie was there and it would look to him as if they were following him out. He saw them and they both quickly darted back to their seats. Ten minutes later they gathered themselves up to leave again, but when they got outside into the harshly lit and noisy street, there was Marnie trying to hail a taxi. They attempted to avoid his gaze but it was too late. He had seen them. At last a cab drew up. 'Night girls,' he nodded, scarcely able to hide his amusement, and hopped in.

'One thing to be grateful for,' Nell said to Laura as they both sat heavily on the top deck of the bus home, 'although we made complete fools of ourselves at least we didn't try to be poetical or anything.'

It was true. Their behaviour had been footling and childish but thankfully they hadn't disgraced themselves further by using the word 'chafe' or 'fronds' and trying to be intimate with him in that way.

There was an interlude of two years between that important first meeting and Nell's next brush with Bill Marnie.

'We've met before haven't we?' she said when they met again, this time in the light rooms of a new building of the college in which he was a lecturer in English literature.

'Oh yes.' He smiled up at her from his armchair. 'So we have.'

But when she knew him well enough to refer to the monstrous embarrassment she had been prey to in Charing Cross Road, Marnie admitted to her, haltingly, that he had no recollection of seeing her that night. That is, he remembered that he had given a reading at around that time and had a vague idea that there had been some life afterwards, some drinking and some girls, but that was all, nothing more. Well, Nell had certainly been piqued at this. 'Some girls!' she said, dealing a mock right hook to the edge of his cheek and affecting a grinning sulk for all of two minutes. But then he had pleaded for forgiveness so appealingly, extolling her manifold virtues: face and grace fortified by supreme intelligence. Nice cook, she added; good in a

74

crisis he recalled, and she had happily let it drop. It was unkind to press the matter further. Nell felt it shook his idea of himself a little that he could have been so careless as to lose such a piece of time. After all, he was a poet and supposed to be so noticing and all.

Their second meeting took place in his study. Marnie was all in blue. He sat in the armchair, serious and smiling, crossword on his lap, cup of tea balanced on one of many piles of books on the floor, saucer level with the cuff of his navy gabardine trouser leg. Nell was early and had knocked on his door ten minutes before the appointed (anointed, she thought it) time of four o'clock. The week before she had written him a letter on her heaviest notepaper in her most frank and elegant handwriting to ask if she could possibly come and chat to him for half an hour to find out more about the course, have a quick look round the college. Marnie answered her letter with a phone call. It came on her seventeenth birthday.

'Nell, there's a Bill Marnie on the telephone for you,' her mother called out.

'Oh my God. Muuuum. Help. Heeelp. Tell him I'm not in.'

'Shhh, he'll hear you. Don't keep him waiting.'

Nell was some time getting to the phone. 'Hello?'

'Hello, Marnie here.'

Everyone called Bill Marnie, Marnie. From Phyllis, the thin, chatty woman who cleaned the rooms on his staircase – 'Why do you always hang your clothes on the floor, Marnie?' – to the Master of the college:

'Marnie, I did like your piece on Keats in *The Times*.'

'Hello,' Nell said.

'And how would Wednesday suit? Wednesday tea?'

'That would be lovely,' Nell answered, feeling a skittish note creep into her voice. She liked talking on the phone, found it less embarrassing than the other way. Marnie gave her some simple directions.

'Hang on a sec, just let me find a pen that works.' Nell raced round the room until she found one and returned to Marnie's mild tones. When he had finished telling her the way she said, 'It's my birthday today.'

'Is it, now?' Marnie said. 'Many happy returns of the day.'

'Thank you very much.'

'I'll see you on Wednesday at four.'

'Right then.'

'Goodbye.'

Face to face with Marnie. Eye to deep sea-green eye with him. As she had entered the room, Marnie, for a joke she could only suppose, or to put her at ease, had picked up the crossword page he was reading and, with exaggerated movements, had thrown it behind his chair and taken up and lowered his eyes onto a ridiculously large and heavy book, affecting the embarrassment of somebody caught loafing. He looked up at her again, the poet and Romantic scholar. But the book was upside down in Marnie's arms. He turned it round the right way. ''S'more like it,' said Nell and they both started to laugh. It was a heroic gesture on his part.

Having told him they had met before, years ago at

the bar in Charing Cross – it was something she had mentioned in her letter – she sat down opposite him, facing a large window. Immediately beyond the window was a low, light-coloured brick wall and then a thin, murky channel of navy water which ran round the buildings, clogged with lily pads and overhung by willow trees. A neat family of ducks was stationed within Nell's view.

Boarding the train at Paddington Nell had felt a sudden surge of nerves about the meeting and had almost turned back. What did you say to someone like Marnie? A friend of hers had been for an interview at a different college the day before and had been asked, 'So are you going to say something brilliant about Words-worth, or not?' while the four men who were questioning her grinned and nudged each other as if they were watching a peepshow. Surely that wouldn't be Marnie's style. 'It's just an informal chat, an opportunity for you to get an idea of the college and whether or not it might suit you. Oh, and don't forget to dress plainly,' Mrs Simmonds at school had said. 'He's got a bit of a reputation when it comes to young girls.'

Once settled in the carriage and leafing through Marnie's book on Keats, Nell wondered again what she would do in the way of conversation. At Cambridge the man who was interviewing Laura had interspersed his questions with enormous, smelly yawns. Because she was brave and because she had had enough, she had said with some archness, 'Do hope I'm not keeping you up.'

'No, darling, but one would always rather be in the

77

bath or at the opera,' he had sighed.

Charming! As the train left Reading, Nell went to the lavatory, washed her face and pinched her cheeks until they glowed pink, as she was looking a bit pale. When she returned to her seat she realized that not only her hand but her whole arm was shaking. Just at that moment a guard passed down the train with a refreshment trolley laden with sandwiches and cake portions, tins of fizzy drink and miniature bottles of wines and spirits. Seeing the man opposite her order a gin and tonic, although she had never drunk gin before, Nell decided to give it a try. The warm, flat liquid slipped down easily. Immediately it calmed her, gave her more colour in her face and lent her a sense of daring.

Suddenly Nell flinched. Marnie was asking her a question. 'What d'you think of the view out of my window?'

A deafening clamour of words, all blind and fumbling phrases suggested themselves to Nell, simultaneously. But she played safe. 'It's lovely.'

'We give people a pretty free rein here, leave them to their own devices, but I imagine that might suit you rather well.'

'Yes,' Nell nodded.

'And are you reading anything interesting at the moment?'

'Been reading a bit of Tennyson.'

'D'you like it?'

'I do, actually. It's much more intelligent than I remembered.'

'Oh, really?' This seemed to amuse him.

'Yeah, I think so, you know.'

'Do you think it's intellectual in any way?'

'I don't know. I suppose in a way it isn't because although he does have ideas, he's not analytical towards them at all. Maybe he is though, I don't know,' she added.

'No, I think you might be on to something there,' Marnie said.

'Would it be wrong to ask you about your work a bit? It's just I'm so fond of it,' Nell was surprised to find herself asking.

'Not at all. I love talking about my work. You mean the poems?'

She nodded.

'Well, what would you like to know?'

'Probably just the things that everyone wants to know; but I mean does it seem a big cost, you know, expensive somehow to wrench all that stuff out of you, painful and unhappy things and make it into a poem? I know you've been asked things like this before, but I mean I just wonder if it does actually hurt you, the doing of it. I'm not saying it's therapy or anything, I can't think of anything worse than poetry written as therapy, but sometimes reading your poems, and your other things, it feels a bit like you've made a quite deliberate cut into yourself in order that things might come out, not spill or anything messy or uncontrolled, but just come out. I don't know, this probably sounds really stupid, but I just sometimes wonder, at the moments when it does seem like a cut, whether you're making the cut so that there can be a poem, or making the poem out of a cut that's already there, as a way of sealing it, or making it worth something more, a happy accident, not happy because it's obviously unhappy, but, d'you see what I mean at all, probably not. I don't know.'

Nell stopped speaking. She felt her face red hot, then looked up at Marnie and he was looking at her, absolutely astonished.

'Perhaps this all sounds completely mad?'

'How old are you now?' Marnie asked her.

'Seventeen.'

'I hope you don't mind my asking, but are you drunk?'

'I was very nervous on the train and stupidly had a gin and tonic, but I wouldn't exactly say I was drunk.'

'I see.'

'I'm sorry,' Nell said.

'Don't be sorry. It was very good, what you said.'

'Oh, good.'

'I'll look forward to reading your exam papers.'

Nell laughed. Marnie stood up.

'Perhaps you'd like some tea.'

'I'd love some,' Nell said.

Marnie disappeared through a door into a small room in which Nell could just make out the corner of a bed. He was gone for some time. Nell heard a tap running and the clinking of china. Then, after another interval, the room in which Nell sat was filled with the old-fashioned tinny rattle of an alarm clock. Marnie re-entered with two small cups of tea.

'I'm afraid I never got round to getting a kettle, but I do have an old teasmaid. Of course it means making tea has become a bit of a palaver, but I rather like that.'

'I like it in *The Dead*,' Nell told him, 'when the young girl suddenly says, "The men that is now is all palaver and what they can get out of you," and for some reason it's really really shocking, because the man, Gabriel or whatever, has just made a friendly enquiry as to how she is or whether she's courting or whatever and that's what she says.'

'I know. It is really shocking. The sudden violence.'

He handed Nell a cup of tea. She said: 'Teasmaids are a great invention and everything, but they're sort of, I don't know, a bit, a bit modest aren't they? They seem almost mechanical rather than electric. And then they're not trying to do anything much either, are they? Well in some ways they aren't because they just wake you up and give you a cup of tea, but then at the same time, that's quite an emotional, quite an intimate kind of thing to do, like what your mum or, or your wife might do. It's funny to get a gadget to do it for you.'

'I can see you've thought long and hard on the subject,' Marnie said, laughing. 'I presume you're not a Goblin employee.'

'No,' Nell said smiling. 'I suppose it's just the gin and tonic talking.'

Everything she said seemed to tickle him, she couldn't help noticing.

'You're a very good advert for it,' Marnie told her. Then he looked at his watch.

'I suppose I should be off.'

'It is getting rather late.'

'Thank you so much for letting me come and see you. I think I will apply here. I can imagine being in rather a good mood here.'

'Well, I'm sure we'd love to have you.'

'Thanks so much,' Nell said again.

'Thanks,' Marnie said. They shook hands and Nell left.

'What a completely mad afternoon,' Nell told her mother when she got home.

'What did you talk about?'

'I don't know. Teasmaids, mainly.'

'Teasmaids?'

'Yeah.'

'How strange. But then, you know how eccentric these academics are.'

When Nell boarded the same train from Paddington nine months later to be interviewed by Marnie's college following what she felt to be a completely disastrous performance in her entrance exam, she had the idea that their previous meeting might somehow stand her in good stead.

With her mother's good luck wishes had come an ominous sort of warning: 'Well, it will make your father's day if you get a place, that's for sure.'

'Why d'you say that?'

'Well, I just think he would be pleased, that's all.'

'Why?'

'Well, I mean, the fact that it's where he went to university, and then you know how he likes tradition and so on, and he's always taken an interest in your education, wanting you to go to his old school, and he's always liked your intelligence.'

'I s'pose so,' Nell said.

Her mother looked at her awkwardly for a moment. She opened her mouth and closed it again. Then she said, 'He did actually ring last night. I wasn't going to say anything until you got back but now that we're on the subject . . . Anyway, he sends you his "very best luck" and says he's sure you'll pass with flying colours.'

'Did he say anything else?' she asked very casually. She liked to counter her father's occasional communications with some indifference.

'Yes, he said he'll ring again in a week or so to see how you got on.'

Marnie was wholly absent from Nell's interview. The four other members of the English department seemed distant and severe, swooping down on her when she said something vague, making her account for her every uncertainly expressed idea. It came as rather a surprise to Nell, then, when a letter came a few days later informing her that she had won a place for the autumn, that term started on 1 October, that she was expected to make considerable progress with the reading list that gave the titles of 800 books and that there was a linen scheme she must opt out of, in writing, if she didn't want to use college sheets and have them changed every Monday.

Chapter 5

Nell had been preparing what she would take to university for weeks before the actual day set for departure. She had arranged all her clothes into several neat piles interleaved with white and pink tissue paper and tied up with mauve ribbons. Twenty-two pairs of pants, five bras, seven vests made one pile. Four jerseys and three cardigans made another. There were two suitcases full of books. The night before term was to begin, Nell's mother presented her with a white towelling dressing gown which she had sewn herself. 'I thought it might help keep you warm. You hear so many stories of students freezing to death.'

On the appointed morning Nell and her mother packed all her things into the car. Just as they were about to set off, the postman arrived and put the day's letters into Nell's hand. A pale blue airmail envelope and a familiar hand signalled a communication from her father. Nell opened the letter, standing on the pavement with her back against her mother's car. A narrow, folded slip of paper fell to the ground and when Nell picked it up she saw that it was a cheque for a thousand pounds.

Dear Nell,
This is just to wish you well. I thought I might send you a similar cheque at the beginning of each term, if that suits.
I'm sorry not to have heard from you but I expect you are very busy with preparations etc.
Best,
Dad.

'What's that, Nell?' her mother called to her from inside the car.

'Some money from Dad.'

'Good for him,' the older woman nodded approvingly. 'Good for him.'

'I s'pose so,' Nell said.

When Nell first set eyes on the room in which she was to live, her heart sank. It was small, musty-smelling, modern, exactly square with no distinguishing feature apart from a poster left behind by the former occupant depicting the face of Sid Vicious with a particularly unwelcoming expression. There was a tiny bed on a wooden ledge which could be pushed into the wall to make a narrow shelf of sofa or extended to its full three feet at night. To the left of this bed that seemed to promise many sleepless nights, and somehow could not have been more single if it tried, was a small desk with two drawers and a Parker Knoll chair upholstered in a sludge-green tweedy fabric. To the left of the desk in the corner of the room by the window was a high-backed armchair covered in the same material. Nell tried both the chairs and the bed in each of its guises. She wandered over to the desk. In the top drawer was a piece of card, bearing the following words in genteel, sloping type: 'If you are sick, it may not be your fault, but if someone else has to clear it up, we suggest that a payment of approximately five pounds is made.'

Piling all her things into the middle of the room, Nell decided to take a stroll round the college. Waving her mother off, there was only one thing in her mind and Nell spent her first afternoon and evening at university wishing she would and praying she wouldn't bump into Bill Marnie. There had been a meeting for all the people in her year and Nell couldn't help immediately knowing that none of them were ever going to be her good friends. There was a shy, spindly boy called Robbie Spittle who had a nice smile, but seemed distant or half asleep. There was Helen, tall, serious and burdened-looking. Rebecca from Huddersfield with hair down to her waist and odd Sunday best clothes on, frilly white collar and kilt and blazer. Two girls, Debbie and Sarah, already seemed to have struck up a lifelong friendship, giving each other constant little nudges and sharing a can of diet Coke through the same straw. Kenny, good-looking but completely terrified, fidgeting nervously and unwinding the wool of his home-knitted cardigan. And no Bill Marnie to be seen.

Nell knew that Marnie was going to be a key figure in her university career. In her daydreams they were already laying the foundations for a grand love affair of historic importance. She would become his muse, and he her mentor. Their romance would at first be clandestine, but in time he would want all the world to know and he would shout it from the rooftops. Yet Nell's hopes, in this respect, were severely dashed when, on her first meeting with Marnie, in the street, he, lean and pale, racing out of the newsagent's with the evening paper under his arm and she all a-fluster crashing straight into him, he did not recognize her. This was quite incomprehensible. She had steeled herself for their first meeting, thinking carefully of the sort of things she might say to him. It had often seemed extraordinary to Nell that she had gushed so when they had met before. Where that surplus of confidence had come from she just did not know. The incident at the paper shop brought her down to earth. What there was in the way of romance between them existed only in her head. He probably made tea on the teasmaid for everyone. It didn't necessarily distinguish their relationship.

During her first weeks at college, Nell spent most of her waking hours in the lower reading room of the university's oldest library. She had made friends with the tall, serious girl called Helen, who was extremely conscientious, and every day the two of them made their way to the library priding themselves on the fact that they were generally sitting on the cold stone steps by nine-thirty when the heavy wooden doors of the library were unlocked.

Helen set the pace for their studies. There would be a two-hour stint followed by a quick coffee in a nearby café attached to a church or a brisk walk around the block. Another two hours of work was followed by lunch, two more hours and it was teatime, at which Helen could sometimes be coaxed into splitting a three-pack of custard creams, then after another two-hour period they would head back to college arm in arm, weary and weighed down by the heavy sacks of books that each girl carried. That October it rained every day for almost three weeks so they were often soaked by the time they reached their tiny college rooms and both girls caught streaming colds. But Helen insisted that they soldier on and they sat in the library wrapped up in many layers of clothing and scarves and gloves, coughing and sneezing, all pink and glowing from their high temperatures. Sometimes in the evenings they went out for a drink with some of the people on their course, Debbie and Sarah, or Robbie Spittle, who had taken a shine to them both.

Sometimes the three of them walked down the street together, Robbie in the middle with a girl on each arm. Hell and Nell. Once he even got up in time to accompany them to the library, although he only lasted two hours, after which he said he had to meet someone about an electric guitar.

Helen liked to cover sheets and sheets of paper with carefully constructed notes in her old-fashioned italic handwriting (she had seen the writing in a book and liked it so much she had decided to make it her own).

She had explained to Nell that she felt it wasteful to read anything without making a detailed summary of what it was about and how it was made and the reasons why it was considered good and bad.

Nell, by contrast, divided her days between searching for rare background material that might shed peculiar light on the texts that she was studying, each day calling up numerous little-known reviews and strange historical documents that would enable her more fully to reach the heart of the writing she admired, and daydreaming. Her daydreams were of a romantic nature, as libraries had always seemed promising to Nell, in this way. Even the local central library at home, with its red plastic seats and fluorescent lighting strips had seemed to hold so many secrets and this feeling was increased a thousand times in the lower vaulted room in which she now sat, with its historic wooden panelling, long oak tables and the low lamps that gave off pools of golden light more fitting to a discreet restaurant than a place of work. In the library, at any moment, a man might spy her at work in her demure grey skirt and jersey and fall in love with her. You saw it happen occasionally. As a boy got up for a break, a girl might happen to get up at the same time, and by chance they'd end up in the same café, at the same crowded table, and then a few days later you'd see them come in to work together in the morning and she'd be wearing his leather jacket.

Nell opened her books. She was looking at an essay by Voltaire on Epic as a clue to *Paradise Lost*, and stopped every few minutes to look up a word in the French dictionary. After some time she shut the book, picked up her pen and started writing.

> *Oh quite attractive girl in the library*
> *You in your old-fashioned typist's clothing*
> *Is it Wharton or Henry James you are reading?*
> *Hair gripped out of your eyes by metal*
> *Ought to wear glasses but you don't*
> *(They might not become you)*
>
> *And you nip out every now and then*
> *For tea, for toast some other assignation*
> *Never long gone:*
> *A man might come in with a question for you*
> *Seeking that book you last had or your hand;*
> *Well may you sit here and will it to happen.*
> *Let's hope it comes before your elbow wears quite through*
> *Meanwhile, sensible, it's work you throw yourself into.*

Nell read through what she had written and counted up the lines. Then she picked up her pen again and drew a thick line through the middle of the page, crumpled it up and continued with Voltaire. Her father had once told her that Voltaire said it took him twenty minutes to talk away his face when he was with a girl. But no one of any interest came into the library all morning. When she and Helen ate their cheese and salad sandwiches in the traffic wardens' café in the covered market that the proprietors had thoughtfully done out in yellow walls and black-and-yellow chequer-ed flooring, Nell despaired to Helen of the lack of love interest. Helen was only so interested, but they did discuss the possibility of relocating to a new library.

Just then Bill Marnie entered the café, saw them immediately and when he had ordered and paid for his food, came over to their table and asked to join them.

The lunch proved to be rather a success. Marnie was in a good mood and laughed at almost everything Nell said. Nell, to her horror, saw herself dissolve into the Royal Variety performance, cracking jokes like there was no tomorrow. Marnie was talking to them about odd jobs he had done to make ends meet while he was a student.

'And then for a while,' he was telling them, 'I had a job as a salesman for a company that made caravan awnings.'

'Oh,' Nell said, 'so you used to go up to people and say, "Look out, look out there's a caravan coming, that'll be five pounds please."'

Nell collapsed into giggles, Helen gave an arch smile and Marnie was laughing so much that he knocked a cup of cold tea over Nell. He immediately cursed himself, sprang up to get a cloth from the lady at the counter, raced back to Nell and was about to start dabbing at her shirt when he thought better of it and handed the cloth to her instead. Nell smiled shyly. Just then the waitress brought Marnie his plate of double egg and chips. The girls finished their sandwiches. Marnie asked them what they were reading and then it was time to go. The three of them left together.

'Well,' Helen said when Marnie was out of sight. 'Will that do?'

Nell laughed. 'I suppose so.'

That first term Nell would come to Marnie's room for a tutorial once a week and once a week she would attend a small seminar group there. Sat amongst the thousands of sweet-smelling books, and the tea cups overlooked by the oil painting of five lemons and a framed faded photograph of Marnie's father in his uniform and medals and a charcoal drawing of a little girl, in full view of the ducks Nell would gaze up at him from her chair. Clothes were strewn across the floor and packs of Lucky Strike cigarettes spilled out of a large, duty-free carton; there was a tangle of two telephones, an old, red Roberts wireless, a stray sock, *Woman's Own*, half a sandwich on a paper plate and then Bill Marnie, his hands holding the essay which she had just read aloud to him.

'It's really good,' he said. 'The individual points you make are original and full of surprises, and the arrangement of the ideas works well.' He referred to a book that he thought she might like and then said he might have it or it might be in London. He scoured the piles of books and the shelves and came across it. He brought it down from the shelf and when he came to open it they found that the pages were still uncut. He took a knife from his desk drawer, gave it a good wipe, and began separating the pages for her. Nell was delighted at this special attention. When the tutorial was over and she was safely back in her small college room, a room that was exactly two floors above the rooms that Marnie occupied, so that her floor was almost his ceiling, she found that she was still holding the chewed red-and-black pencil with the pinkish rubber on the end that Marnie had been writing with. She thought of taking it back to him, right away, but it would make her ridiculous. Instead, she decided to keep it somewhere safe.

All the girls in the first year had crushes on Bill Marnie. It was a joke with the male students in the college that if you wanted to get inside the knickers of a female English student you had to compete with Bill Marnie's bloody halo. They just could not see the attraction. Marnie did not cut much of a figure walking across the quad in one of Oxfam's best suits, his brown lace-ups with their permanently unravelling laces and his trade-mark unironed shirt. He wasn't rich. He drove a clapped-out sky-blue diesel Ford Fiesta. He ate in workmen's caffs. He did appear occasionally on the TV, but only at some unearthly hour with other sad, unknown writer types.

Throughout Nell's first term the vision of Bill Marnie travelled with her wherever she went like a benign ghost. Working alone in her small college room, sitting under the light of the Anglepoise by the window that rattled in the wind and at night, Nell watched Marnie smiling down at her from the sky. She saw his face appear in the slick porcelain of her wash basin when she cleaned her teeth at night. Her thoughts turned to him if she saw a man of his height (five foot ten) or when a man in brown lace-up shoes went by. She had taken to calling him Brown Shoes in her thoughts, as his name, Marnie, sometimes seemed too hard for her to say. On buses she remembered and recited his poem about sitting on the top deck ('Upstairs, Downstairs'), the narrator drawn to the suspended street scenes below (a very young mother and a baby, two women OAPs with tartan shopping trolleys, a teenager wrapped round a cider bottle, a lone traffic warden) and gripped by the horrific arguing of a couple on board who were tearing each other apart. When it hailed she thought of his poem 'Hail' and agreed that it was oddly comic that particular type of weather, all dry and hard, so that people often laughed when they found themselves caught up in it.

In the street Nell was often convinced that she had seen him approaching and was forever darting behind corners, swerving up alleys, bundling herself into shops and racing up library steps to avoid bumping into him. But when she emerged from these random buildings and passageways, the man in question was almost always some inferior being. Relief and disappointment followed these phantom sightings, and also embarrassment which trebled if the episode occurred when she was not alone.

'I think you're in love with him,' Laura wrote to her from Cambridge. Laura had found herself a serious and sexy boyfriend of her own age, leaving the giggling bookshop days firmly behind her.

'I am not in love with him,' Nell insisted time and time again. 'I'm IN CRUSH. It's completely different.'

'That's right!' Marnie's face gazed up in agreement from a rainbow that shimmered in an oily puddle. 'That's right.'

Crushes in the abstract, in practice and in theory, were of interest to Nell. She was an expert on the subject. Since toddlerhood she had freely attached herself to a variety of individuals, pinning her hopes and dreams onto an odd collection of men and women with some degree of abandon. She would look up to them, blindly copying their dress, championing their causes, following them about and confiscating their minor personal effects. She made friends with their friends to authenticate the connection.

Nell's first crush had been on the milkman. He brought her lollypops that turned from black to red to green to verucca yellow when you sucked them. Then there was Mrs Merritt, the helper at her nursery who told Nell to her face that she was the most beautiful girl in the under-fives. Then there was Mr Farthing, a severe and grudging English teacher who once gave Nell 104% in a test because she had included some essential information that he had neglected to take into account when setting the questions. And then there were the feelings she had nursed towards her father.

Since his departure for America, Nell had tried to cut Richard Fisher out of her life. If she pictured him in her mind's eye she made an effort to strip him of his impressive bearing, reducing him to a dwindling figure with sloping shoulders and a shifty expression that bore witness to his own sense of the shabbiness of his behaviour. Gradually Nell weaned herself off the need, the desire to talk of him, or think of him and what he meant, resolving vaguely not to keep in touch, dodging his phone calls and leaving many of his letters unanswered. She did, however, read them. Fisher was a good correspondent. He wrote regularly and made a point of including her in his perception of what he sometimes referred to as the New World.

I went to the Old Town Tea Rooms today, I think you might rather like it there. They had 99 different kinds of tea and enormous stodgy cakes. They bring you a plate of them when you sit down and you just help yourself. I was there for about half an hour, just reading the paper in the evening, and I had three almost without noticing. I could hardly move afterwards. When you come I'll bring you here and we'll have a competition to see who can eat the most cakes, but I'm afraid I'll win. Then afterwards we'll go on a long slow walk until we feel healthy again.

Nell imagined herself being sick in a series of Boston's fanciest toilets and shook her head. If I do not reply for long enough, the letters will stop, she said to herself. It's all show. He doesn't want to look bad. Now and then, she would pick up a pen and write the sort of letter she would send him if he hadn't gone away and they still had their old life together. In these letters she spoke of her friends, her adventures, new things she had come across in her reading.

> *Had I the heavens' embroidered cloths,*
> *Enwrought with golden and silver light,*
> *The blue and the dim and the dark cloths*
> *Of night and light and the half-light,*
> *I would spread the cloths under your feet:*
> *But I, being poor, have only my dreams;*
> *I have spread my dreams under your feet;*
> *Tread softly because you tread on my dreams.*

These letters Nell kept piled up in an old grey shoe box.

Twice since his departure, when she was fourteen and just before her sixteenth birthday, they had met for lunch in London. For Nell these were highly strained occasions, but Fisher seemed to sit easily with her, enquiring politely about her studies, offering her considered advice over chargrilled fish and straw-coloured wine. After each of these meetings Nell wrote a brief card of thanks, not seeing the communication as an overture, but merely as a basic, unemotional politeness due even to a stranger. If Nell was at home when Fisher called on the telephone she would speak to him, even cheerfully, if her spirits were good, but it was important to her that she never made a move to contact him. When he had suggested these two meetings, or made any other sort of a request of her (he once asked her to buy and send him a medical journal) she would acquiesce, but it made all the difference to Nell that she never actually started anything herself. When she was seventeen she finally made the decision that thinking about Fisher, talking to him, seeing him, was exhausting and unsettling to her. It was easier to be without him completely than to have him in tiny dribs and drabs. When Fisher's letters dwindled almost to nothing, birthday and Christmas cards, perhaps a phone call or two in a year, she was more able to untie herself from him. But sitting loose from him brought its own problems. The many hours she had spent at first examining their conversations and the minutiae of their relationship, and then, steeling herself against these thoughts, were all returned to her empty and looming.

Nell dreamed that Marnie imagined her undressing, kicking off her shoes, coyly slipping into her pyjama bottoms before unzipping her skirt and leaving it empty on the floor. She saw him watch her sleepy-eyed climbing into bed, smoothing down the covers. She thought that he might come and see her and perhaps speak to her or touch or kiss.

At the moment he was lecturing on colour words in *The Eve of Saint Agnes*. Nell had made the point, at their last meeting, that many of the colour words were in fact colouring words, describing changes, new shades. You were shown the colour as it became a colour: 'flushing', 'Made purple', 'Rose bloom fell', 'blush'd'. She herself had coloured when talking to Marnie on this subject. She was afraid that any show of embarrassment whatsoever would surely betray her feelings for him so she tried to adopt a matter-of-fact, no-nonsense approach.

When she had first arrived at university the college doctor had summoned her for an internal examination as was the practice with all new women students and so, for the first time in her life she undressed in front of a man. She had not wanted to seem faint-hearted or babyish at the prospect and to convey this to the doctor she had whipped off her skirt almost as soon as she was through the door with a cavalier pretence of no shyness. After all, he was a doctor and saw thousands of bottoms and willies and fannies every day, she thought. When he had said, 'Well, we'd better have a look,' she had smiled and whipped off her pants as if it was the most ordinary thing in the world, taking off her knickers for a man, for the first time. What she had wanted to say was, as it was noon, 'I don't want to put you off your lunch.' Nell could see that the speed with which she had made herself naked in order to demonstrate her ease with such things had made her a bit comical. Afterwards she was anxious that he might think her over-keen to have him see her in the nude, to have him look at her in what he referred to as 'that department'. Because her attitude to nakedness seemed so casual, she feared her behaviour implied that having clothes on was actually rather a strain for her. She had gone too far the other way, replacing the silliness of embarrassment with the ridiculousness of zealous nudism. And then, because her attitude was so matter-of-fact the doctor had been none too careful with her feelings. He fed her feet roughly into the stirrups and grunted, 'Part your knees.' When it was all over he had soaped his hands for all of two minutes and she felt cruelly stung by this. It was the first time she had opened her legs to a man and it had struck him as a health hazard. However much she told herself it was standard practice guaranteed to reassure her of his fastidiousness, of his having done the same with the person before her, it still felt like a slight.

Nell talked brashly and carelessly to Marnie about the flushings and blossoming in the poem that was their subject; then, to make the conversation as unintimate as possible, she had adopted a tone so flat that Keats's robust, intricate dreamings were made to sound as ordinary as cheese.

> *Into her dream he melted as the rose*
> *Blendeth its odour with the violet –*
> *Solution sweet.*

In an attempt further to kill any romance, Nell said, 'It makes me think of Iago's description of Desdemona and Othello's kiss,

> *– They met so near with their lips*
> *That their breaths embrac'd.'*

Marnie looked puzzled at this and vaguely amused. 'When you think of something lovely does it automatically conjure up something unpleasant?'

This was rather a personal question. 'No, not really,' Nell answered.

'Good,' said Marnie. 'It would be more obvious to think of Lorenzo and Isabella:

> *– Parting they seem'd to tread upon the air,*
> *Twin roses by the zephyr blown apart*
> *Only to meet again more close and share*
> *The inward fragrance of each other's heart.'*

The hour was up. Someone else was hammering on the door for his attention. This was the sort of thing Nell dreaded, parting when there had been talk of parting lovers, and doomed parting lovers as well. She said goodbye to Marnie. He must know, she thought, he must know by now. She hadn't got the balance right here either and she felt as humiliated as when she was lying, prone, on the cold stretcher with her feet in the itchy stirrups in the doctor's surgery. Nell was longing for Marnie to really notice her, to single her out, and take her in. But not in this way.

Chapter 6

Halfway through the term a new girl arrived to read English. No one was quite sure why she had missed the beginning of the term: a holiday, an operation, disillusion with another course. Nell's year was not told, just asked to welcome her and help her to catch up. Olivia Bayley had an impressive bearing, a graceful, willowy form, fine large features, deep blue-grey eyes, tall narrow legs, a tiny waist, a long straight back and she carried round this charming argument for English beauty with convincing diffidence. She smiled a lot and occasionally stammered as if to show she was half amused by the blessing and half embarrassed by the burden of these great good looks.

As term progressed and her feeling for Brown Shoes became stronger and harder, Nell's confidence dropped to an all-time low. She felt rundown and exhausted, shivery, anxious and drab. The arrival of Olivia, Nell took as a cruel blow. She viewed the girl through Brown Shoes' eyes and Olivia's very existence grated on her soul and brought the object of her desire crashing into her thoughts much more often than she would have liked. It seemed to Nell that all the considerable advantages that could be boasted by her own person were far exceeded by Olivia's, who was taller and more graceful. There was more than a hint of great ancestry and tapestry-hung castles about Olivia, generations of pointlessly tall relations fed on roast beef and ladies with world-famous bone structures and icy reserve. She was altogether more distinguished looking than Nell, who felt like the comely but clumsily built kitchen maid compared to the king's own daughter. Nell heard in the bar that Olivia had done a few fashion shoots for *Vogue* while still at school, but, being so shy (everyone was always saying how shy she was) she had found it rather painful and had decided to give modelling a break for a while. To make matters worse Nell had come out in a number of boils, one on her bottom, two on her shoulder and the most vicious being on the instep of her right foot, so that once or twice she found herself hobbling along behind the charmed Olivia's untroubled strides. When she returned to the doctor, feeling altogether more timid this time, he had prescribed a course of antibiotics which cured the boils but had the nasty side-effect of bloating her stomach so that her clothes stretched tight across her middle.

Nell liked to dress plainly, but she felt garish and hideously 'got up' compared to the simple, uncaring clothes Olivia wore. Olivia's garments were somehow anonymous. They could have been vastly expensive or they could have come from a jumble sale. This kind of artlessness seemed ostentatious to Nell and also aggressive, as if it were behaviour deliberately directed against her.

In the next few weeks of term, however, it transpired that Olivia was an unforbidding soul despite her appearance. She was often to be seen in the college bar drinking almost exclusively with male students. She liked to talk and it became known amongst the handsomest of men in the college, who kept abreast of such matters, that if you could only stay awake long enough to keep the conversation going when all the others had run out of things to say and sloped off to bed, then you could usually see her back to her room. Nell was certain that Brown Shoes must have seen Olivia and fancied her. It would have been impossible for him, for any man, not to.

'How are you settling in?' Marnie asked her one day.

Nell had bumped into him in the high street and they were walking back to college together.

'There hasn't been such a good year for a long time. We'll be hoping for a lot of firsts,' he said.

'I'm fine,' Nell said. 'Everyone seems very . . . very nice and friendly.'

'They're a good bunch,' he laughed.

'And that new girl . . . ' Nell started.

'Olivia Bayley?'

Nell fell silent at the sound of the girl's name. Marnie was not giving anything away, but he did look hard at

Nell when she said, 'I think she's the most beautiful girl I've ever seen.'

The next day Nell met Brown Shoes in the quad. He was wearing old grey plimsoles and looked about seventeen.

'Hello there,' Marnie said.

'Hello.'

'You walking into town?' He was smiling so she nodded. Actually, she was on her way to the college library in the opposite direction. They walked along together. Her boils were back again and she had a little difficulty keeping up.

'You still limping?' Marnie asked. 'That's nearly four weeks, isn't it?'

'It comes and goes. It's got a bit infected, but I'll just have to go on antibiotics again.' She was touched as well as sorry that he had held her ailment in mind.

'You must be a bit run down.' Marnie was looking at her face. They were turning into the high street. At that moment Olivia Bayley sped past on a bike, then stopped and wheeled herself back to where they were standing. She was carrying a large bunch of flowers wrapped in cellophane across the handlebars, looking the picture of health in baggy, pale grey drawstring trousers and a holey thick linen jersey.

'Hello Nell, hello Marnie,' she said. A boy went past on a bicycle and wolf whistled at her. Olivia flushed and stammered, 'Hhhhhh how are you both?'

'Fine,' Marnie said.

'I'm fine as well,' Nell said.

'Good. I am too,' added Olivia, lowering her eyes modestly. She's so affected, Nell thought. They were standing at the corner.

'I suppose we should all be getting on.'

'Byee.' Olivia cycled off and turned to give them a wave.

'Byee,' Nell called after her kindly.

'You don't like that girl, do you?'

'I certainly try to like her,' Nell answered after a while.

'I shouldn't let her get to you.'

'I can't help it.'

'Well, I don't know why,' he smiled cheerfully and Nell took heart.

The next day, Marnie was four minutes late for the talk he was meant to be giving in the large seminar room in the Benjamin Cranley building. Most of Nell's year were already seated round the horse shoe of chairs and tables that furnished the room. Entering the room, Nell caught sight of Robbie Spittle. He was tapping on the glass of his wrist watch with a look of mock severity. Nell smiled at him and sat down. He grinned back at her.

'Hi there,' he said.

'Oh, hi. How are you?'

'Yeah, I'm pretty good, I'd say.'

'Oh good.'

'How about you?'

'Yeah, you know.'

'What you been up to?'

'Not much, just jigging about vaguely. Nothing exciting.'

'You're looking great. Tired, but great.'

She laughed. 'Thanks. You've really made my day.'

'Anytime.'

She had washed her hair and put on a shirt that she had bought with Brown Shoes in mind. It was a man's pale grey Vyella shirt with mother of pearl buttons, which fitted her loosely apart from across the bust, where the fabric was slightly strained. Brushing her hair she had made her parting further to the side than usual and she had secured her whispy, brown growing-out fringe with a sandy-coloured hair grip. Shirt and hair-do, she felt, gave her the look of an ardent librarian. Womanly and self-controlled. Just right. The rest of her was dressed in a grey woollen A-line skirt, which fell to within three inches of her knees, and dark tights and shoes. Her face had looked more colourful than usual in the mirror this morning, livelier and somehow lit up by the first traces of an extremely good mood.

Marnie walked into the room absently with a large pile of xeroxes, which he began to distribute amongst his class. When he handed Nell her share of the papers she blushed immediately and dropped them all. Together, they bent down to pick them up from the floor and the side of their heads gently knocked together. Nell's blush deepened. 'God I'm so sorry,' she said.

'Not at all, it was my fault entirely.' Marnie smiled

graciously and went back to handing out the texts.

When the xeroxes had been distributed Marnie said, 'Hazlitt thought *King Lear* was the play in which Shakespeare was most in earnest. What do you think he meant?'

That night, circling her fingers round the place on her forehead where his head had knocked into hers, Nell started compiling a list of all the things she liked about Marnie. Halfway through itself, the list suggested a name to her, 'Marnie's Nobilities'. It was eleven o'clock. Nell changed into her night clothes, collected a pen and paper and a hardbacked copy of *The Wasteland* on which to lean and got into bed, propping herself up with pillows. Even as she wrote, Nell knew that the document she was creating was entirely an exercise in ludicrousness, but at that time the ludicrousness of the thing was exactly its justification. After all, it was by denying something, by squashing and pouring scorn on it and the circumstances from which it arose, that you landed in trouble. If you allowed a crush, wallowed in it, turned it into a bit of a carnival, made his movements and mannerisms into big songs and dances or mentally hoarded his nicely turned phrasings and his tender, shy looks, then the power of the thing got reduced, made into slapstick and horseplay, a bit of a joke, a game. With this sort of treatment, a degree of feeling that was potentially crippling became just an adjunct of other girlishnesses. 'Marnie's Nobilities' was completed. This catalogue of attributes was especially important to Nell because it gave her liking for her tutor a certain ordinariness. If there existed facts which proved attractiveness, in the abstract, then the extremity of your own liking was given a rationale, its obsessive quality was, in part, explained away.

Nell analysed Marnie's character in two separate columns, firstly in terms of the things he said and then with reference to certain key incidents which had involved him, as if he were an invention in one of the books she was studying. He was an invention to some extent, but Nell was conscious that she didn't only swoon and pine for him in a vague, old-fashioned way. She desired him fiercely, in her arms and in her bed, large as life and real as meat, as tears.

The list of virtues had twelve headings:

Manner	the way he treats everyone well
Grace	he sees the good in everyone
Genius	for poetry, for criticism and for beautiful behaviour
Generosity	with his knowledge and ways of thinking
Friendliness	makes you feel important and valued
Knowledge	unending
Words	precise, well chosen, enlightening, humorous
Confidence	quietly authoritative and strong minded
Modesty	not self important, v. interested in others
Intelligence	natural, gained through life
Wisdom	and gained through reading

| Scholar-liness | high quality of his academic output, knows about all new ideas which affect his subject, not afraid of theory, nor a slave to it |
| Phys. Attributes | esp. eyes, smile and Brown Shoes |

The list completed, Nell compiled a brief negative catalogue of behaviours that Marnie could never stoop to. Top of this list was *deceit* followed by *plagiarism*, *malice* and *being boring*.

Nell looked at the time on her alarm clock and saw that it was three o'clock in the morning. She felt buoyed up by her writing and certain she would be unable to sleep. She tossed and turned at some length, finally drifting off ninety minutes later, pen still in hand.

Nell awoke, read her list, edgily, and decided to issue her crush with an ultimatum. It was beginning to get painful. She would give herself up to it completely for two more weeks and if she still had not made any sort of progress she would call it a day. It's good to try to legislate over matters of the heart in this way, Nell told herself, but it's not natural and she knew there was a chance she might not be able to rid her thoughts of this presence which dominated them so thoroughly. It would be interesting to see what would happen when she attempted to exert her will-power to this end. At ten o'clock Nell went to Marnie for her weekly tutorial.

'I'm sorry.' Nell could see Marnie was in the middle

of something. 'Am I a bit early?' She knew she was on time. She always was.

'No, you're exactly right. I just thought that I had a bit of an idea about something.'

'I could easily come back later.'

'No, come in. I thought I had something, but it's nothing. Just baby-talk.'

'Baby-talk?'

'Yes. I thought it might lead to something. I had this idea sketched out, but it'll keep.'

'You'll have to put it on toast for a couple of hours.'

'That's right.' Marnie sighed and then his face brightened.

'Is it driving you a bit mad?'

'What, writing?'

'Yeah, I mean I've read, I know, that some people really hate doing it.'

'I do hate it.' Marnie smiled. 'But I love it as well.'

'Oh, I see.'

'I mean, when it goes well it makes me feel better than anything else.'

'I can imagine,' Nell said.

'It's as if with the words I'm trying to say to someone, "Here I am," and then I read back the words and very very occasionally there's something worthwhile and I have made an actual poem, or think I have as opposed to a mess or something that's too deliberate sounding or whatever and if it is a real poem, when I read it back instead of my saying, "Here I am," suddenly the poem says, "Yes, there you are."'

Marnie stopped talking. He looked absently across the room, to the ducks in the water and beyond them to the golden-leaved trees.

'God, it's so interesting,' Nell said.

'Well it is and it isn't.' Marnie smiled. 'Anyway, have you got anything for me?'

Nell drew her essay out of her bag. Wouldn't it be awful, it suddenly occurred to her, if she had brought him the other document instead, the one from last night. She was very embarrassed by the many pages of writing. 'I'm sorry it's so long,' she added.

Marnie said nothing, but he didn't flinch at the length. He began reading her work, stopping every so often to pencil something in the margin.

Marnie laid down her essay after several minutes. 'It's good, Nell. Very well written as always, and you make some fresh and lively points, but the idea isn't an invulnerable one. It might be wise not to confine yourself to such a small area next time.'

'I see,' Nell said.

'It's interesting what you say about Cordelia, that we're hardly told anything about her apart from the fact that she was her father's favourite and that she won't play a part, that she takes a stand against poetry to a certain extent. Did you think at all about how this differs from the play's source, where we're told that she is "so nice and so demure/So sober, courteous, modest and precise" and also that she looks more fetching in the new fashions than either of her sisters and this is why they dislike her?'

'No, I didn't,' Nell said.

Marnie talked her through the comments he had written, then her hour was up. There was someone else knocking at the door. It was Olivia Bayley. Nell gave her a brief smile and went back to her room. I wonder if he talks to her about his writing, she wondered.

That evening she added to 'Marnie's Nobilities' three further sections. There was a list of the people he admired (Nietzsche, Patrick Kavanagh, Molly – the college secretary . . .); an inventory of the items of interest in his room, as far as she could remember them; a folder containing press cuttings concerning him, including some of his book reviews and assorted pieces of journalism, many of which Laura had kindly surrendered from her former collection.

The next night, Nell made a point of writing out her six favourite poems of his and composing a poem of her own.

As time keeps very quietly
I wish up for a time that we
A person and a person in a place may be
With rings of similarity
And checks and bouts and poetry
To complement our industries

Oh don't think it's I can't/won't see
You absolutely properly away, and richly
(I'm a bit involved myself – it seems)
And then, we're none of us at all unhappy
Though one day, unhanded and the worse for wear we might be

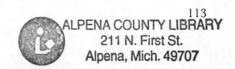

And yet, not blue, not even green, just quietly
And this (and that [and you]) amazes me.

And then, suddenly, Nell's crush was completely out of hand. It persecuted her through her dreams, where shady figures exacted impossible dues from her or offered her things she wanted only to whip them away again when they were within a hair's breadth of her grasp. During the day it accompanied her heavily wherever she went, chastizing and humiliating her in turn. What you want you can never have, it said, laughing at her. If you were more this, if only you were more that, you might have it, but you aren't I'm afraid.

Occasionally it became specific. If you looked like Olivia Bayley; if you had some subtle and modestly owned genius for writing or an incredible talent for sexual intercourse, but as you are? No, I don't think so.

But when these thoughts came, and she looked in the mirror at her virgin frame and bashed at her head with her fist, it seemed to her that she wanted Marnie more than ever.

Previously, the anxiety of Nell's position had been underwritten by enough faith in a vague and distant togetherness with Marnie to sustain a little romance. But now the romance had dwindled down to nothing and a large amount of drudgery had taken its place. The crush had originally shared some similarities with a graze or minor injury, which it was pleasant to prod or squeeze and feel warmed and distracted by the sensation produced. These feelings had long gone.

When Nell's mind turned to Marnie now, not that it ever really focused elsewhere, it no longer imagined her drying dishes in a bright kitchen with lots of colourful enamel saucepans and dashing off the odd novel while he wrote poems in an adjacent dim study under a golden pool of lamplight, or sexual intercourse verging on the holy, with her fitting him like a glove. No, Nell's own grasp on the situation was becoming so tortured that all she could reach towards in her mind was one thing: his name. She said it over and over again as she tried to sleep and when she awoke it was her first thought. And the two short syllables of longing made her whole body ache, as though her arms had been fixed in a permanent stretch towards him. There was a new, sheer quality to the pain and it hurt all the time. When Nell actually saw Marnie now, it was so difficult to reconcile the enormity of her relation to him with the thinnish, untall man who stood before her, that she left his company feeling not just confused, but actually as if she had been slapped.

Laura had tried to get Nell to see sense. 'This is turning into an obsession, Nell. I've been thinking about it a bit and it seems to me that obsessions happen when a person has a large vested interest in not thinking about something else.'

'I don't know.'

'So all you need to do, then, is think about the other things and the force of this will lessen.'

Nell was silent.

'You're making yourself ill.'

'I know I am.'

'You do look lovely, but you don't want to get any thinner.'

'I know. I just keep being sick all the time.'

'Are you making yourself sick?'

'I don't know.'

'You don't know?'

Nell was crying now. 'It's all such a mess. I've worked myself up into this enormous state and then I start choking and then I'm sick. I'm so disgusted.'

'It's so bad for your health, Nell.'

'I know.'

'Of all the ways of expressing yourself, it has to be one of the very saddest.'

'I know. I hit my head as well.'

'Against the wall?'

'With my fist.'

'Oh, Nell.' Laura wrapped her arms around her. 'I can't bear to think of you doing that. Your poor head.' She stroked Nell's head with the back of her fingers.

'What am I going to do?'

'I think you should see a doctor.'

'I can't.'

'Well, I don't think you really have a choice. We'll go together. You've got to sort this out, Nell. What's your doctor's number?'

Laura picked up Nell's address book.

'He's really horrible.'

But Laura was already dialling. 'It is serious yes. No, I don't think we can wait till the morning,' she told the

116

receptionist and Nell was given a cancellation for that evening.

At five-thirty Nell and Laura were seated in the surgery waiting room. There was a low table with tattered copies of women's magazines and a small, brightly lit rectangular fish tank containing one solitary fish.

'Nell Dorney?' the receptionist called.

She went in, refusing Laura's offers to accompany her, and sat down with the woman doctor. The man who had been so disgusted by her genitalia was thankfully on holiday.

'There's nothing really wrong with me. It's just that I'm in a bit of a state,' Nell said. 'I don't seem to be able to sleep and I keep banging into things and I can't stop thinking about my tutor and I haven't done any work for weeks and I keep throwing up all the time.'

'How long have you been feeling like this?'

'Oh, I don't know, quite a long time. Three or four weeks.'

'Have you talked to anyone about your feelings?'

'Well, there's my friend Laura, but I didn't really know . . . '

'Would you like me to make an appointment for you to see a counsellor?'

'I don't know. I don't really go in for that kind of thing.'

'I think it could really help you.'

'D'you think?'

'It'll probably be a week or two to wait and I'm wondering what we can do for you in the meantime to get you through.'

'I don't know. I don't suppose you could give me some tranquillizers?'

The doctor shook her head. 'I very much feel that isn't the answer for you at the moment. Perhaps you'd like to tell me a bit more about what you're feeling. Does your family know you're having difficulties?'

'No, not really.'

'Perhaps you ought to let them know . . . '

Leaving the doctor's room with an appointment to see a counsellor in two weeks' time and half a diazepam for that night, Nell collected Laura from the waiting room.

'You seem very very tired,' Laura said.

'I'm completely exhausted.'

At seven o'clock, Laura tucked Nell into bed with a mug of cocoa, a hot water bottle and some magazines and then together they administered the neatly halved yellow pill.

'I'm going to have to get back now. I wish I could stay, but I've got this big essay due in tomorrow evening. Ring me if you feel bad. I mean it, Nell. Even if it's four o'clock in the morning,' Laura said. 'And if it's an emergency I can probably get Rob to drive me, so we could be with you in, I don't know, two, two and a half hours.'

'Thanks so much. You're being so completely brilliant. It's making a real difference. I feel terrible, putting you to all this trouble.'

'Listen, mate, you just concentrate on getting better. It's no trouble at all. I just hate to see you so unhappy.'

'I don't feel so bad, you know.'

Laura left her to sleep. Nell was mildly soothed by the drink and the pill and imagined it doing her some good. She felt calmer, but at the same time less tired, more lively.

At ten past eight Robbie Spittle knocked gently on her door.

'Come in,' she called out wearily.

'Hey, Nell,' he said, 'early night?' He came and sat on the end of her bed. Robbie was dressed in faded black cotton trousers and a black jersey with three thick grey stripes running down the front of it. He had had his hair cut short.

'You all right?'

'Yeah, just knackered.'

'You don't fancy coming to a party, then?'

'I probably shouldn't.'

'Quick drink, then?' He pulled a half bottle of whisky from his bag and took a swig and passed it to her. Nell took a swig herself.

'Has your friend gone?'

'Yeah, she's got an essay to do for tomorrow.'

'Oh right. Nice girl.'

'The best.'

Robbie passed Nell the bottle and she took another gulp. The whisky was completely delicious.

'So what kind of day have you had, Robbie Spittle?'

'So-so.'

'Yeah?'

'Yeah.'

'You sound a bit sad.'

'It's nothing. It's just that . . . ' Robbie's voice trailed off.

'What's up?' Nell said. Robbie remained silent.

'There's this person . . .' he began slowly.

'Is it someone you like?'

He nodded.

'Tell me.'

'She's special,' Robbie said and grinned.

'I see.' Nell looked at his face but now he was looking away. 'Can't ask for more than that.'

He passed her the whisky again. 'I dunno.'

Nell sat up in bed and straightened her pyjama top. 'This whisky is just what the doctor ordered.'

'Funny doctor you must have.'

'I went to see her today.'

'Yeah? Everything OK?'

'Yeah. I'm just in a bit of a state.'

'Join the club.' He drank again from the bottle. 'No, but I do hope, you know, that everything's OK. I really do. I mean . . . ' Robbie went quiet.

Nell took another drink. Robbie seemed in a world of his own. Nell watched him gazing mournfully towards the window and the dark trees.

'You all right there?' she asked.

'Yeah, fine.'

'Yeah?'

'Yeah.' Nell took his hand. His eyes still fixed away from her, Robbie said softly, 'Nell?'

'Yeah?'

'Look I know you're feeling down and everything and it's really bad timing but I . . . ' He turned to face her and their two mouths met up in a kiss. Robbie gently folded his arms round her. He kissed her softly and stroked the edge of her hand under her stripey pyjama sleeve, back and forth, back and forth. He put his hand to Nell's face and felt the skin of her eyelids and her ears and her neck. Tears ran down Nell's cheeks. The room had grown dark. Nell closed her eyes and wriggled down into the bed. Robbie was lying at her side, on top of the blankets.

'You all right?'

'Yeah, fine,' Nell whispered. 'You?'

'More than all right,' Robbie answered. She opened her eyes. Robbie was looking at her, 'You're so lovely, Nell.'

'You're not so bad yourself.'

They must have drifted off to sleep like that, hand in hand, because when Nell opened her eyes it was eleven o'clock. 'Robbie?' she said softly.

'What?' He yawned and lifted his head up from the bedspread.

'So, we going to this party, then?'

'Yeah? You coming?'

'What have we got to lose?' Nell asked. 'Just give me ten minutes to get changed.'

'Nice one. I might slip into something a little less comfortable myself.'

'Woo,' said Nell.

Robbie went back to his own room for a bit, promising to return shortly. Nell got up and put on the black mohair mini dress that she kept for best. She put on black tights and shoes. Then she took everything off and put on the grey skirt and shirt and jersey she had been wearing earlier. Tentatively she moved towards the mirror in the corner of the room. 'If I'm not mistaken,' she said out loud, 'you actually look quite good.'

Robbie knocked at the door and came in. He was wearing the same jersey with a different pair of black trousers. 'Nice one,' he said, looking at her. They made their way out of the college buildings, across the quad, passing through the porter's lodge. Nell was a little wobbly on her feet.

'You're drunk!' Robbie said, surprised, taking her arm to steady her. 'Did you and Laura hit the bottle earlier?'

'Yeah, cocoa,' Nell replied. 'Oh, and half a tranquillizer.'

'Housewife's special, eh?'

'A heady cocktail of drink and drugs,' Nell said. They both laughed and walked off slowly up the London Road.

'Where is this flaming party anyway? Reading?'

'We've only been walking for four minutes and twenty-two seconds.'

'You must be joking. We just passed a field of cattle,' Nell said, pointing back to The Master Butcher.

'Yeah, right,' Robbie said. 'Nearly there.'

'Bet I won't know anyone.'

'You'll know loads of people.'

'That girl will probably be there and you'll blank me in the corridor. I know your sort, Robbie Spittle.'

'We'll see,' he answered, passing her the whisky bottle. 'We'll see.'

'I can't believe how delicious this is,' Nell said. 'It makes me feel like a girl again.'

'Know the feeling,' Robbie said and his hand crept round Nell's waist and rested on her hip for the remainder of the journey.

'I knew you were going to say that.'

'I knew you knew and I didn't want to let you down, or anything.'

'Oh, shut up. Let's have a bit of hush at the back. Thank you, move along the bus.'

'You're off your trolley.'

'Ah, you say that to all the girls.'

'I don't, actually. Here we are,' Robbie said. They turned into the front garden of a small terraced house and Nell rang the door bell.

'Do you hate me?' Nell suddenly asked.

'No, I lo—' But there was no time for declarations.

'Hi Robbie, hi Nell. Come in. Clare's invited her bloody tutor, can you believe it? So half the party now feels guilty that they're not at home writing essays.'

'What did she go and do that for?' Nell asked.

'Bit of a crush on him, I think.'

'Original,' said Robbie.

'Who's Clare anyway?' Nell asked.

'That short blonde girl in the second year.'

'What subject?'

'Same as us.'

Nell and Robbie stepped into the kitchen and came face to face with a wry-looking, dishevelled, smiling Bill Marnie.

Chapter 7

Nell could not speak but Robbie was jovial and talkative enough for two. The whisky and the pill suddenly lost their effect and Nell felt the impact of all her earlier dread. She could not look at Marnie; she could not even listen to what he said. She would have liked to have returned his smile, but instead she ran out of the room up the stairs and locked herself in the bathroom, where she was sick into the toilet bowl. She flushed the chain, wiped the seat with some toilet paper and washed her hands. She looked at herself in the mirror above the basin and dabbed at her face with some wetted tissues, then she splashed it with water. She looked surprisingly healthy under the circumstances, her cheeks glowing pink from their walk. Nell sat down on the bathroom floor. She could slip away from the party and get a cab home, but it would be mean to leave Robbie, especially as he was being so nice, and Laura had been amazing; even the doctor had been kind in a brusque sort of way. Nell unlocked the bathroom, switched off the light and let out a tiny cry of fear and delight. There, sitting at the top of the stairs waiting for her, with a cigarette between his lips, was Marnie.

'Are you all right there?' he said gently. 'Robbie and I were a bit anxious.'

Nell attempted an attractive smile and came and sat next to him on the stair.

'I'm fine,' she said, and took a deep breath. For the first time in two weeks she trusted herself to look at him and she was disappointed at what she saw. He looked cold and pallid and sad. Someone turned the stereo up and now the house was vibrating visibly with the sound of music and dancing. The ceiling above their heads, shiny cream paint, cracked, peeling and streaked with nicotine stains, began to shake. A small amount of fine white dust fell down onto their heads. 'Do you think it's all right?' Nell said pointing upwards.

'I would have thought so.'

'I can't help feeling you look a bit sad,' Nell said.

This comment startled them both as they were not on these sort of terms. Marnie looked up and smiled.

'I suppose I am a bit sad,' he agreed, 'but no sadder than the next person. I'm very drunk,' he added.

Nell said, 'I suppose I'm a bit sad, too. But I hate the idea of you being unhappy. I mean, for what it's worth.'

Brown Shoes laughed at this but added seriously, 'What's making you sad, then?'

Nell took a deep breath, 'Oh, you know.'

Marnie nodded understandingly. After a while he said, 'I mean, there are certainly things that are

126

working sadly inside me at the moment, but they're controlled sadnesses, I'm quite strict about it, usually I am anyway.'

'Oh yeah, I am too,' Nell said. 'Only way to be, really.'

They were quiet for a few moments. Nell tried a new tack. 'Are you reading anything interesting at the moment?'

'Chaucer, Keats, John Berryman.'

'I suppose someone might say that they follow on from each other a bit.'

'That's exactly what I am saying,' Marnie laughed. 'What d'you think?'

'Obviously I know almost nothing about it, but I'm sure it's completely right.'

'I might give a talk on it in a couple of months' time.'

'I hope you do, I'd be really interested . . . '

Someone turned the music up again and now it was impossible to carry on talking. They could dance, but somehow Nell felt it would be indiscreet with half the college looking on.

Marnie was writing words down on a piece of paper. He put the paper into her hands. The words said, 'Shall we slip off?'

Nell nodded and they left the party and drove off in Marnie's car.

Nell awoke in Marnie's bed. It was nearly six o'clock. He lay sleeping heavily by her side. Nell was still in all her clothes: vest, pants, tights, shirt, jersey, skirt and bra. She had removed her coat and gloves and scarf and shoes and they lay in a pile at the end of the bed. For a moment Nell wished she was wearing these outer garments also. Marnie had no clothes on. Nell's hand lay lightly across his back as he slept and his skin felt much warmer than hers, despite her battle dress. Nell, in fact, was shivering. Marnie might wake up at any moment and be cold to her, not in any deliberate way, but simply by not seeming pleased to see her. She tried going back to sleep, but it was impossible. When they had fallen into bed the night before, Nell soft and shy by this time and Marnie frank and serious although drunk, he had said, 'Are you really going to keep all your clothes on? Won't it be very uncomfortable for you?'

'No, it's fine, I often . . . ' Nell's teeth were chattering, but Marnie was kissing her and Nell felt grateful that he hadn't insisted she remove her clothes, nor had he taken it personally in any way. She had unbuttoned her cuffs and rolled up the sleeves of her shirt and jumper to the elbows and Marnie was stroking her face and neck and her forearms a lot, perhaps because it was the only skin that showed. Kissing Marnie, Nell felt very small. Until very recently, night and day she had dreamed about Marnie, about him loving her and earnest sexual intercourse, after which he would say important things to her about his work. And she in turn would feel ashamed at the enormous gaps in her reading: Dryden, Trollope, Defoe, Virgil . . . the list was endless. Despite these dreams, when Marnie cupped Nell's breast and made little circles with his finger round her nipple through the two layers of cotton and one of wool and kissed it, and when moments later Nell's calf accidentally brushed the outline of what must have been his erection and her eyes darted immediately up to his face to see if this had registered – and it had – she felt in danger, out of her depth, a kind of vertigo, and she said almost inaudibly, 'I think we should say goodnight now.'

'If you like,' Marnie said, 'but you must promise me some kisses in the morning.'

'I promise,' Nell said. 'Cross my heart.'

'We'll say goodnight in a minute then.'

About an hour later they said goodnight. Just before, Marnie tucked a lock of stray hair behind her ear and planted a kiss on the middle of her forehead. 'You looked so demure in your grey clothes.'

'I wanted to look like a librarian on her day off.'

'On her night off,' Marnie corrected her.

When Marnie awoke, he did not seem especially pleased to see her, but instead rather heavy hearted and aloof. More kissing seemed out of the question. Nell asked him if he was all right and he answered her, she felt, irritably, 'Of course.' Nell rose and got herself a drink of water and came back to bed with it. Marnie had gone back to sleep. If you made someone promise to give you something, did that mean you promised to want it, did it oblige you to accept it, somehow? Nell had tons of kisses all ready for Marnie but he seemed not to want them. She got up and put on her coat and scarf and shoes. In the pocket of her coat were gloves and she put these on too. She wrote on a piece of paper, 'Gone home as feeling a bit funny, love Nell,' and put the paper on the floor by the door. She walked in the dawn from his room, across the quad out of the college gates and down the long misty road until she reached the high street. There was no one about. She lingered on the bridge, rubbing her hands together to keep warm. The air around her was white with cold. A clock struck six. There were early signs of life now, the odd car, an occasional person on early shift, very enthusiastic joggers. Nell sat down for a moment and gazed up at the sky, which was beginning to clear. After a few moments she saw a tramp approaching her. It was a man she often stopped to talk to. Nell stood up and smiled. They chatted for a while.

'You all right, pet?'

'I don't know.'

'Ah, you'd know if you were.'

'Well, I suppose I'm not then.'

'Nice girl like you. Need someone to look after you. Wandering the streets at all hours.'

'I know.'

'Breaking your heart over some beast. Am I right?'

'I don't know.'

'Oh, you'd know all right.'

'OK. Better head off,' Nell said.

'Don't forget now,' he called after her mysteriously.

Nell retraced her steps back to college. All she could think was she mustn't bump into Brown Shoes. She had to pass his very door to get to the stairs that took her back to her own room. Once out of danger, she got into bed, still in all her clothes, and fell into a deep sleep.

All day long, Nell banned herself from thinking of Marnie. The second that a memory of their evening came to her, Nell bursting into tears after being sick again in his bathroom and not telling him, Nell opening her eyes in the night to see Marnie looking at her and saying she looked very tired but very beautiful, him kissing her fingers and stroking her neck. Just as she began to survey these thoughts, Nell forced her mind onto other areas, other problems. She needed to choose a subject for her dissertation, to decide what to buy for her mother's birthday. She wondered vaguely about how she could be more healthy, what to do about Robbie. She winced now to think of their kisses. She had definitely blown it with Marnie, made herself completely ridiculous by keeping all her clothes on and creeping off without saying goodbye, and then all that talk of sadness. What must he think of her? Behaving like a fourteen-year-old convinced that everyone wanted to jump on her. Nell shooed away the discomfort, drowning out her thoughts with the sound of her voice, reciting over and over again a cautionary tale she knew about a boy who was eaten by a lion, as if it were some sort of prayer. She sighed, vastly disappointed in herself, putting her happiness in the hands of a man on the very day she had decided to do everything in her power to wash him out of her hair. Just as she was beginning to imagine that she might one day become immune to Marnie, that she actually wanted to free herself of his drain on her resources, she had risked everything on one mad spree.

There was no sign of Robbie. He must have put two and two together and was probably disgusted with her. She'd have to make amends to him in some way. The whole thing was a mess. She wanted to recall some of the sweetness of the night before, but she was terrified of getting a taste for it. But, she was not sorry. At least she had had one night with him; for God's sake they had stayed up half the night kissing. She would always remember it, in the future, when she didn't feel so at risk over it, but not now. She couldn't afford to think of it. What had he thought of it, of her? She should have made more of an effort in bed. It was a great mistake not to have. He must think she was complacent. He had said three times that he thought she was beautiful. When he had looked at her there was something so soft in his eyes and in the way he kissed her that it had seemed very moving. To behave in such a loving manner and not mean it would actually be cruel. If only she knew what he thought. She shook her head at the picture of herself trying to be sexy in five layers of clothing. To flaunt yourself as an object of desire and then when it came to the crunch to go all limp and shy. When she was a child there was a face she sometimes made, she thought it made her look grown up, sophisticated, alluring and now and then she pulled it in front of the mirror when she was on her own. She practised making this face, and spent many school playtimes searching for an object worthy of this look. When she had settled on Joseph Wright, she practised even more, perfecting the glance, the quizzical available slant of the eyes, the half smile, half curl of the lip, the soft inclining of the head. When the great day came, Nell sat in the classroom before school, waiting for Joe, lost to the world as she practised her special look, twisting her mouth into a variety of contortions, when suddenly to her horror she realized he was watching her, watching and grinning broadly. He moved towards her, gave his shoulders a shrug in her direction, tentatively reached out his hand towards her and gave her two soft pats on the top of her head before racing into the playground to tell his mates.

Nell went back to sleep and awoke at five p.m. when there was a knock at her door. It was Robbie. She let him in and he came in and sat on the end of her bed.

'Where did you get to last night?'

'I suddenly had to go. I was really tired. I did try to find you.'

'Yeah?'

'Did you have a good time?'

'It was OK.'

'Yeah?'

Robbie was smiling shyly. 'You seem to be spending a lot of time in bed these days.'

'I know. It's just where I like to be at the moment.'

'You coming to the pub later?' Robbie asked her quietly.

'You know I am,' Nell said. There was a hint of irritation in her voice. She had forgotten that

Robbie's band was playing tonight.

'Well, maybe we can have a drink after the gig, yeah?'

'O K.' They both fell silent.

'Look Nell . . . Last night, I, I mean, I didn't want you to think . . . '

'Let's talk about it later.'

'Yeah?' He looked at her.

'What time are you on?'

'About half eight.'

'O K. I might have a bit of a sleep before then. I'm exhausted.'

'You will come, though?'

'Promise.'

Robbie closed the door, leaving Nell to sleep. 'See you later then, Babe.'

Robbie's band, The Mod Cons, was doing its first proper gig that night at the Aldgate Tavern. Nell had never heard Robbie sing before, apart from one night when she and Helen had stumbled home drunkenly from a party with him shouting, 'Show me the way to go home' at the top of his voice.

When Nell arrived at the pub it was empty. She had often passed the long narrow building and heard it pounding with heavy metal, spilling men in leather and studs and girls with orange hair into the street, but she had never been in before. The pub was dank and smelled of cigarette smoke and drains. A middle-aged woman was sponging down tables and straightening chairs. She wiped down a stack of ashtrays that sat on one end of the bar and distributed them, still smeared with grey, amongst the tables. The pub was dark, but one or two orange bulbs shed a dingy light onto the table tops, just strong enough to reveal the sticky film of spilled alcohol and the beads of water left behind by the barmaid's greasy cloth.

'What can I get you?' the barmaid asked Nell.

'Whisky.' The barmaid poured from a kingsize bottle into a tiny metal measure.

'Better make it a double,' Nell said. She sat down on a stool and rested her elbow on the damp bar.

'Come to see the gig?'

'Yeah, my friend Robbie's on about half eight. The Mod Cons.'

'Tall, short dark hair, is he?'

'Very skinny,' Nell added.

'I know. Very popular with the girls, that one. Very popular.'

'Oh really?' Nell smiled. 'That's interesting.'

'Yes, very popular indeed.'

'Well, he is a dark horse then.'

'Why, you two, er . . . '

'Oh no,' Nell said. 'Friends . . . '

'I see.' The woman disappeared briefly behind the bar and popped up a moment later with a can of air freshener.

'It's disgusting in here,' she said to no one in particular, spraying the fragrance of summer meadows into the corner of each room. The three distinct scents of beer, ash and toilets dissolved into a more nauseous smell of vomit. Nell held her breath.

Then Robbie appeared. 'Nell!' he said and kissed the inch of skin between the corner of her mouth and her cheek.

'Hi! What you drinking?'

'Snakebite?' Robbie asked the barmaid.

'We don't serve that, I'm afraid. Attracts the wrong sort of punter.'

'Oh, go on,' Nell pleaded.

The barmaid sighed and filled a pint glass half with bitter and half with cider.

'Magic,' Robbie said.

Nell paid and bought another whisky. The bar was beginning to fill. Girls in mini skirts and pastel T-shirts that stretched tight over their bosoms. Robbie surveyed the room. 'My fans,' he said, with a trace of mock swagger in his voice.

'Yeah, right,' Nell answered, but she couldn't help noticing the girls eyeing him up, eyeing her.

'Better nip off,' Robbie said. 'I'll catch you after, yeah?'

'OK.'

The barmaid leaned over to Nell across the bar. 'You're well in there, love,' she said. 'Well in.'

Nell smiled. It was eight-fifteen. With any luck she'd be home by ten. She should have brought Helen out, but Helen was probably still in the library, it being before midnight. In the last few weeks things had been going badly between them. With the approach of exams, Helen's morale had collapsed. She had grown increasingly edgy and competitive. The day before, she had burst into tears because Nell had managed to track down an obscure structuralist essay on *The Canterbury Tales* and had referred to it in passing to Helen, who was unaware of its existence.

The pub was half full now. Two young men had joined the woman behind the bar. Suddenly there was a hush, a loud cheer followed by whistling and high-pitched shrieking from the largely female audience. The Mod Cons, all apart from Robbie, had appeared on the tiny platform at the far end of the room by the gents'. The four boys, lean, tall and pale stood cradling guitars and pint glasses, smoking and looking moody in their scruffy clothes. There was another huge cheer as Robbie walked out onto the platform, taking his place centre stage and whispering something to the drummer.

'I love you Robbie,' came a high-pitched voice from a girl with bleached blonde hair in bunches.

'Cheers for coming down, yeah?' Robbie responded.

The girls cheered again, then fell silent.

Robbie's unaccompanied voice began humming a low note, a rough crash of drums followed, there were a few short moments of silence, and then Robbie Spittle opened up his large, expressive mouth and started to sing his heart out. The song was so loud and fast and frenzied that it was almost impossible to listen to. In the song a boy was persuading a girl to come home with him, using all his masculine wiles, all his mod cons as a lure.

> *I'm gonna wave my magic wand*
> *I know I may not be James Bond*
> *But I've got (drumroll) ALL the mod cons.*

The girls and some of the men at the front were pogoing up and down up and down as each chorus came. Nell was amazed. On stage, Robbie was transformed. Suddenly he had become completely unselfconscious, heroic, razor sharp. On the tiny platform, adjacent to the toilets, ripping every last drop of energy out of his skinny frame, Robbie seemed charming, glamorous, sophisticated, altogether in his element as he jutted his head forward as if heading a football, and looked out amorously into the audience. The man in the song was trying to lure the girl out of her party dress by turning up his new imitation log-effect fire.

> *I'm gonna wave my magic wand*
> *And though I may not be James Bond*
> *I've got ALL the mod cons.*

Robbie's emphasis on the final line varied so that the phrase had become loaded with meanings that ranged from top of the range audio equipment, to contraception to sexual technique, to seduction scenarios and effective methods of deceit. He is a dark horse, she thought. No wonder he wanted her to come tonight. He was a real star, Nell thought, and grinned.

An hour and a half passed without Nell giving Brown Shoes a single thought. She congratulated herself on her nerves of steel until she remembered that the three double whiskies she had drunk might have something to do with it. Robbie was beginning another song, called 'Pick 'n' Mix'. He clasped the microphone to his chest and looked out into the audience half mournful, half ecstatic. 'I think this one's for Nell,' he said. Nell blushed crimson and then suddenly everything hit her, the whisky, the doctor, the night she had spent in Marnie's arms. Her eyes filled with tears.

> *Pick 'n' Mix*
> *Pick 'n' Mix*
> *Your sweet selection's*
> *So fantastic*
> *Your black magic*
> *Your milky way*
> *You're so soft-centred*
> *I'm jelly, Babe.*

Nell looked at her watch and saw that it was five past nine. She put down her glass and went to the toilet, where she was sick. She washed and dried her face and decided to leave. It must have rained while she had been in the pub because although the sky was clear, the pavement was damp. It was only a short walk back to college.

Helen was standing at the bottom of the entrance to her staircase.

'Didn't you go to Robbie's gig?'

'Yeah, it was great, but I came back, I was sick. I need to have a lie down.'

'You OK now?'

'Yeah, thanks. I thought you might have come along

tonight. I know Robbie was hoping . . . '

'I've just got back from London.'

'How was it?'

'It was nice. My parents' twenty-fifth wedding anniversary.'

'How lovely.'

'There was a bit of a party. It was really nice, actually. Did you go to Clare's party?'

'Yeah. It was OK.'

'Apparently Marnie was there.'

'I saw him. He seemed fine.'

'He was looking for you earlier.'

'Looking for me?'

'Yeah, about seven. He asked if I'd seen you.'

'Did he say anything else?'

'No, just that he wanted to ask you something.'

'Oh. I wonder what that's all about.'

'I told him to leave a note on your door.'

'Ah, well, the plot thickens.'

'Anyway, I better get back to the library. Do you want to have lunch tomorrow at the Bell?'

'I'd love to.'

'See you there about one, then.'

'Great.'

They both lingered for a moment, uncomfortable and tentative.

'Look Nell, I'm sorry about yesterday.'

'No, I'm sorry. I didn't mean to upset you. Let's forget the whole thing, shall we?'

When Nell reached her room there was a small white

envelope stuck to her door with Blu-Tack. The note inside said, 'I'll be in the bar at the Northgate. Marnie.'

Nell ran a brush through her hair, changed her shirt and ran as fast as she could to the high street. Flushed and breathless, she entered the bar, where Marnie was waiting. The minute she saw him she felt such a bolt of panic that she lost her footing and bashed her leg into the sharp edge of the chair and came close to falling over. Marnie must have seen her stumble and she was too embarrassed to look anywhere near him, let alone to kiss him hello or even greet him with words. There was a thin red mark on her calf that was already beginning to turn into a bruise. She sat down, head sunk and shoulders curled over her body. Marnie poured her a drink from the bottle of red wine on the table. 'I'm so glad you came.'

Still she could not look at him.

'You look marvellous.'

She shook her head and said, quietly, 'No.'

'Still feeling funny?'

She opened her mouth to speak, but no words came. She tried again. 'Bit,' she said.

'Is it to do with me?'

'No, no.' She was shaking her head again, and put her hand up to her cheek. 'I'm just in a bit of a muddle at the moment.'

'I hope it's not serious. Are you worried about work, because if you are, there's absolutely no reason to be.'

'Not really.'

'Will you have dinner with me?'

Nell nodded.

Marnie caught a waiter and asked if it was too late for a table in the restaurant. He led them through into the enormous dining room, which was empty apart from an elderly couple who were dining in silence. 'I shouldn't think the food's any good here.'

While they were eating, Marnie came back to the subject. 'I hate to think of you being unhappy in any way. You're so robust and lively.'

'I don't feel very unhappy just now, not at all.'

'Good.'

'In fact,' Nell said, her mood lifting as she spooned thick soup into her mouth, 'I feel quite the reverse.'

'I do, too. I can't tell you what a treat this is.'

Marnie picked up a piece of grey lamb on his fork. 'I don't even mind the food being inedible,' he said.

Nell laughed. She had laughed when the waiter in his tail coat had arrived with their food under great silver domes which he had whipped off with some ceremony.

'I don't even mind that this room is criminally over-furnished, that the waiter has trodden on my toe three times, and he's quite a hefty chap, and that it's freezing cold.'

They sat silently for a while drinking and occasionally tugging at a bit of meat. Marnie's expression had altered. Something inside him seemed to be working sadly now. They had both given up on their food.

'Could I twist your arm to come and have a little drink in my room?'

'Yes,' Nell said and her face indicated to him that

little twisting was required.

He hailed a cab and in moments they were inside Marnie's rooms. It was very warm there. A glass jug filled with blue hyacinths and eucalyptus leaves gave the study a strong, fresh scent.

'Sit down,' he said, shifting some books and papers from the velvet armchair. Nell did as she was told while Marnie lit the gas fire. He took a seat in the chair opposite her. Nell looked around the room. 'The first time I met you I warmed to you. I thought, that girl's got a layer of skin missing.'

Nell was too embarrassed to look at him. 'But you didn't remember the first time we met, in that book-shop, when I was in my school uniform.'

'No, my darling,' Marnie said. He was at her side now and she stood up to face him. He leaned over to kiss her mouth. 'I think I'm falling in love with you a little bit.'

'Oh God,' she whispered to herself, as his hand crept inside her shirt and reached for her nipple. Nell closed her eyes. 'But you don't know me.'

Marnie was stroking her hair and kissing her cheek. 'Nell?' he whispered. 'Nell?'

'Hello, Marnie,' she answered him. 'Hello.'

'What are you feeling?'

'I feel good.'

He led her into the bedroom. At the sight of the bed, Nell froze. 'Is it all right, if it's, if it's the same as last night?'

Marnie let out a comical low howl and then sighed. 'It's fine, absolutely fine. Whatever you like.'

In the morning, the pair of them were wreathed in smiles. On waking, Marnie had whispered into her ear, 'Can I see you tonight?' Nell nodded. 'What would you like to do?' he said and immediately she blushed.

'I don't know,' she said. 'We could do lots of things.'

'True,' he said. 'We could have a lovely dinner somewhere and then we could come home and I could tell you stories until you fall asleep. Or we could go and see that new print of *Casablanca* and come back here and get some Chinese people to bring us delicious things to eat. Or Weeee could . . . drive up to London, take in a show and have a cocktail in a rooftop bar afterwards. We could fly to Paris and watch some can-can girls dancing and take a stroll in the moonlight. WE could . . . go and have a drink in the pub on the corner that has Irish music and sink a few pints of Guinness and dance a jig along the length of the Bullingdon Road.'

'We could . . . buy lots of flowers and walk up to complete strangers who look a bit sad and give them great big bunches and shake their hands for no reason at all except that we're in good moods.'

Marnie leaned over and kissed her. 'We could go to an Elvis Presley convention,' he suggested.

'In disguise,' she chipped in. 'OR . . . ' she said, taking his hand, 'We could . . . go to a supermarket and, you know, buy things and cook them. Or,' she continued, 'we could . . . we could pretend that you're a soldier in the army just got back from war and you've been missing me and you come home and you've got twenty-four hours' leave . . . '

And Marnie was kissing her and she was kissing him and all thoughts of soldiers and cocktails and supermarkets suddenly fell away. Nell felt Marnie's fingers stroking between her legs and his mouth on her neck and his arm smoothing her forehead and his eyelashes tickling her chin and his toes wriggling amongst her toes. 'There are so many lovely things for us to do,' he whispered to her, 'and we'll do them all.'

Marnie had to get an early train because he was speaking on a radio broadcast in London. Nell left Marnie's room at eight and took a stroll round the college grounds. Although there was a light frost on the ground, the sky was bright blue and the sharp sunlight made her blink. Nell stood, looking into the distance, drinking in the calm. Then she heard someone calling her name, behind her. She swung round and there was Robbie.

'Nell,' he was almost out of breath. 'What happened to you last night? You just disappeared. No one knew where you were. Thank God you're all right. I was so worried.'

'I'm sorry, Robbie,' Nell said. 'I'm so sorry.' And then both of them realized that tears were pouring down Nell's cheeks.

'What's the matter? What's happened?'

She bit her lip and looked down at the ground.

'It's Marnie.'

'Marnie?'

'I was with Marnie.'

'Marnie?' Robbie said. 'Marnie?' And then slowly he understood. 'Oh, Nell,' he said. 'Oh, Nell.'

Chapter 8

When Nell and Marnie were an item, well, to themselves they were an item – they made sure no one apart from Robbie knew – Marnie told Nell that Olivia Bayley had come close to making a pass at him one evening.

'The dirty beast!' Nell said. She was holding a saucepan full of boiling water and two soft-boiled eggs and so was in quite a strong position. They were having their fifth breakfast together – Nell was keeping count – this time at his tiny London flat. 'Were you tempted?' Nell fished the eggs out of the pan and spooned his into a yellow egg cup and hers into a cardboard bit of egg box which she had fashioned into a makeshift container. She handed him a piece of toast.

'No, not really,' he said.

'You were a bit, then?' Nell inclined her head and gave him a saucy look.

'I find her a bit much.'

'Too beautiful?'

'I certainly wouldn't say that. I think it's all that

breeding. I find it slightly sour. It kind of makes me feel like starting a revolution or something!'

'Ah, you're just humouring me.' They both laughed.

'She's rather promiscuous as well, it seems. And as you know, it's love I want, not syphilis.' Nell put down her spoon.

'How do you know that?'

'Ah – my students confide in me. They come to see me grinning from ear to ear and I ask them, "What's new?" And they say, "I've just spent the night with the most wonderful girl in Oxford,"' he paused, 'or words to that effect, and generally it's her.'

'It might be me.'

'It could be, yes, but generally it isn't you they are speaking of. Thank God.'

'It doesn't surprise me. She is incredibly beautiful,' Nell said. 'I feel like the back end of a bus standing next to her.'

Marnie frowned. 'That's not even good conversation.' He reached over across the table and kissed her on the lips.

'Urr, eggy kiss!' Nell shrieked and she came round to his side of the table and he pulled her onto his knee and they kissed some more. But Nell was intrigued. 'So what happened when she tried to have her way with you?'

'Well, she came to my room late one night, must have been after ten, and she looked a bit dishevelled, not all her buttons done up and so forth, and she'd got a bit wet in the rain coming across the quad. Anyway, she asked me a few questions about Keats and then drew a chair very close to me, sat on it, yawned once or twice, said she was exhausted, a bit drunk, and stammered and giggled a bit, you know in that shy way she has . . . '

'And . . . '

'That's pretty well the long and short of it.'

'Nothing else?'

'Yes. After a while she left.'

'God, you're vain!' Nell said and took a teaspoonful of egg and pressed it against the end of his nose. A little yolk adhered to his left nostril and the remainder fell onto his trousers, leaving an oval, greasy mark.

'Thank you, darling,' Marnie said and went to change. Nell followed him and they went back to bed for a bit. 'This is the life,' Marnie said.

'I know, I'm thinking of changing my name to Riley,' she answered him.

When they got up Marnie had another egg and another piece of toast while opening his mail. A letter from his agent enclosed two reviews of his last book *New Poems*, which had been published several weeks earlier. 'How are they?' Nell asked. Marnie handed them to her.

There are many poets today writing about emptiness and contingency: the uglinesses that are an ordinary part of living life. Bill Marnie's achievement is to find a sort of beauty in these quotidien disappointments. Even the nullity in his poems has a sort of enchantment. It often seems that each word is weighted with the sense that what the poet wishes to find in the world goes against the grain of what the age in which he lives requires from him. Poems like 'Love III' and 'The Haunting' reveal a luxuriance in romance that is constantly turning, now asserting itself, now withdrawing. Marnie knows and constantly shows that a story can tell us a good deal about life, even when fantasy and daydream lie at its heart.

What perhaps is even more impressive about New Poems *is that Marnie keeps us consistently interested in him, wanting to know what he is like, to have him before us so we can see into the heart of the 'I' of his poetry, always wishing to know more. For although Marnie is forthcoming about himself, in his work the texts themselves seem so meticulously made and so well finished that they retain, for the poet, a large degree of privacy. The poems themselves do not build an accumulative picture of their writer, they do not have this sort of continuity, rather each new poem ('Morning', 'The Apparition') seems to start afresh, wholly freestanding and independent, the slate wiped clean for a new picture . . .*

'It's a rave,' Nell said.

'Look at the other one,' Marnie told her.

Bill Marnie's latest collection New Poems *is a sad little book. In many of the poems the writer, whose two earlier collections showed such promise, makes the biggest mistake a poet can make, he doesn't even sound as though he means it. The words are tired and limp, the images flat and dull, the whole lacking in any sort of energy or sense of life. In the poem, 'The False beauties proceeding from art and the true ones from feeling', as we are wearily hauled through academic in-jokes, shop talk and gossip, it is impossible not to feel we are the victims of a self-indulgent exercise in creation, a poor one-liner extended to the length of a sonnet.*

'Blimey,' Nell said. 'I don't think I'll read any more of that.'

'We liked the same girl once,' Marnie said simply. After a while he added, 'I thought we might go to the library this morning. Have you got anything you could be getting on with?'

So the two of them, in coats and scarves with bags of books underarm, trundled off to the library. Marnie's flat was near the British Museum but he preferred a large private lending library in Piccadilly. Inside, there was an atmosphere of amateur scholarship. Marnie explained the set-up to Nell. No one quite did anything serious there. Around ten, ten-thirty, a few old boys arrived. You might imagine that their wives had thrown them out of the house and said not to come back until teatime. So they turned up at the library, all shiny faces and good intentions, and with the ambitiousness of morning time hunted out some Greek texts with the thought that they mustn't lose this particular discipline from youth which, after all, they were rather proud of . . . But the Greek was harder than they remembered, and virtually forgotten already, and after a short period of battling with it, realizing they had bitten off more than they could chew, they put down the book and before they knew it they were having forty winks. It was true: dotted round the library were old men snoring with piles of heavy books at their sides, intermittently waking up with sudden guilty starts, rustling their pages loudly, as if to assert the seriousness of their endeavours which their behaviour itself could not help but bring into question. Then on waking at twelve-fifteen or so, they deemed it hardly worthwhile to embark on another stint, and so they would retire to a nearby café (which was, it transpired, owned by the library) for a long lunch, where the trick was to get on the right side of sharp and mysterious Angela, the most severe waitress in London. This was much harder to do than it seemed and scarcely worth the bother, for if you did make a hit with her she would express her liking by overcharging you. Crushed or cheated, two-fifteen would see them safely reinstalled in the red leather seats at the library, reading the newspapers and the *Spectator* or the *TLS* and then it was a slow walk home, calling in at the pub perhaps, en route, or strolling aimlessly down Jermyn Street with an eye open for a pair of shiny shoes or a new shirt. 'Or a pretty face?' suggested Nell. Some of the men, perhaps, had not even told their wives that they had taken early retirement or been made redundant, Marnie said, going off to work each day and using the library as sanctuary or home from home.

Nell and Marnie worked for two hours and then they went for a cup of tea at a nearby café.

'Do you want the nice café with the beautiful but slightly scary waitress and filthy tea; the horrible, dirty café with the angelic waitress and delicious tea, or the average café with average tea and average waitress.'

'Beautiful scary waitress,' said Nell.

'Good choice.'

The café was Italian and located in one of the alleys that ran between Jermyn Street and Piccadilly. The waitress was short-tempered and had a look of Sophia Loren. When they sat down, she said, 'You be quick because we near the lunch rush and you only order cheap food.'

Nell and Marnie both nodded seriously and she almost smiled and said to Marnie, 'New little friend?'

Nell looked up sharply. 'Ah, touchy lady,' she said and winked and went to get their order.

'She's rather theatrical today.' Marnie looked apologetic.

'So I see,' Nell said. 'So, d'you make a habit of having romances with your students then?'

Marnie ate a crumb of the macaroon he had ordered and washed it down with some tea. 'Absolutely not,' he said. He was serious now.

'Good,' said Nell.

'Although there was one girl,' Marnie looked thoughtfully into the distance and began telling her of an earlier involvement he had had with someone he was teaching.

Eighteen years ago, before his marriage to Jacqueline during the final year of his PhD, when he was occasionally allocated odd hours of teaching by a member of the faculty who believed in him, there had been a tall, red-haired Irish girl called Cathy who fell for him at a time when he had found himself desperately lonely. It was the Christmas holidays and both of them had stayed up in their college accommodation for the whole of December, neither quite having anyone to enjoy the festivities with – Marnie's father and mother being dead and Cathy's family having emigrated to New Zealand four years earlier. College was deserted at this time. It seemed to Marnie that he and this funny girl were the only two inhabitants of the grim and frosty complex of grey buildings that framed the quad. He had invited her back for a drink with him one evening purely on the strength of a silly joke she had told him and some admiration for her colouring and she had made it clear that she would like to be kissed, would quite like to go to bed with him.

What Marnie knew about sex at this point, he told Nell, was a mixture of what he had learned in the few tentative and frustrating romances he had embarked on and the results of his parents' efforts to see him right in that area. Marnie had imagined the scene exactly in his head. One night Mr Marnie senior had been in bed with a book about roses and a glass of milk and his wife had been at her dressing table putting a brush through her long thick hair. It tangled easily and she had to take up a comb and clutch the brown strands a couple of inches from the ends and use the fine metal teeth to scrape out the knots, which she had teased down from the roots with her fingers. Her husband liked to watch her doing this, he had often confided to his son, especially when she worked at the hair at the back of her head and stretched her arms behind herself like wings so that two tender hollows were made between neck and collar bone and her bosoms were raised. She caught his eye and his smile in the mirror as she combed away and said, 'You ought to talk to him about girls, Jim,' and Jim, who never argued with her, nodded and looked seriously at the ceiling for some moments.

The upshot of this was that Marnie had been given a talking to and, more effectively, a book his father had been keeping for him. The book was called *Life Long Love*, it had a pale green cover and had been written in the thirties by a doctor, as a guide for newly weds. Before he went to sleep that night Marnie read:

> *Having undressed, the wife should lie quietly on the top of the bedspread . . .*
>
> *The husband should now gently kiss his wife for a few minutes, ceasing if he feels over-stimulated and inhaling deeply to recover emotional composure. The kisses should become more passionate and should rove over the body, not necessarily being confined to the facial region.*
>
> *When Drake heard that the Spanish Armada was in sight he kept his head and finished his game of bowls. In motoring under new or treacherous conditions it is wiser to reduce speed by taking the foot off the accelerator than to jam down the brakes and possibly skid. So in sex, take it easily.*

Cars and ships and kisses on the facial region mingled

in Marnie's sixteen-year-old dreams as he slept, but the idea that stayed with him most firmly was that it was essential that there was a bedspread if this sort of scene was to take place. His own bed at home was sheets and blankets only. Perhaps there would be a bedspread for him when he got to university. (He had ticked the box on the accommodation form that opted him into the linen scheme and had almost finished the reading list and work he had been set: write an essay on three different books by the same author, showing how the author's style and imagination developed, asked the examination question. Fifteen-year-old Marnie wrote, 'When Joyce wrote *Ulysses* he was rewriting *Paradise Lost* and when he wrote *Finnegans Wake*, he was rewriting Shakespeare.')

But Cathy was passive and unconfident, ashamed of the garishness of her red hair, especially her bright orange pubic hair, and with a sheer terror of pregnancy no matter how many separate precautions were taken between them. She missed her family badly and often spoke of the way Christmas was celebrated at home in Ireland with all the family to which there were new additions every year, relatives descending from America, new babies, in-laws, priests, friends, friends of friends who had nowhere to go. Then there had been three Christmases in New Zealand, barbecues and picnics on the beach, paddling, pulling crackers with her gran in the sea. Marnie's Christmas present to her, seeing as his financial situation, though tight, was easier than hers, was a phone call to her family in New

Zealand from his phone for as long as she liked. He had no idea of the cost of such a call but felt that the present was so right that it would be worth any amount of money. She spoke at length while he sat and read in the other room, having closed the door, but when she came in to him she was tearful and silent. It seemed that his gift had made stronger her longings for home. He cursed himself for not having considered this. As Christmas morning progressed she became sullen and hardly seemed to respond at all to anything that he said, sitting, heavy, in a world of her own, and Marnie began to wish he had given her a different present altogether or nothing at all. (She had given him a sky blue shirt which he was now wearing.)

Things did not pick up between them and Marnie despaired of their getting through the day together. They shared a bottle of Asti Spumante and some cold roast chicken and Stilton and chocolate cake (the Christmas dinner he had bought the day before) and still Cathy remained uncommunicative and dull. The unfairness of her behaviour given his efforts to make everything as nice as possible between them made him chill towards her. The red-and-cream complexion that had seemed lively and healthful to him previously now seemed coarse and comic. Finally he realized that if he did not have some time alone he was going to go mad. But it was Christmas Day. To send her away would mean her sitting in a room sixty seconds from where they presently were, on the other side of the quad where she would be unhappy and alone. Their affair dragged on over the next few days. They sat together in silence and kissed and tried to make love when their loneliness with each other or drink overwhelmed one of them into a dim and modest desire.

When New Year's Eve came, a night which Marnie already loathed because of the intense pressure to be happy, Cathy could not stop crying, nor would she say what was wrong. Finally, because he was obviously getting angry with her, she told him: her boyfriend in New Zealand, to whom she was engaged, had been killed in a car crash on Christmas Eve. He had been driving home with the family's Christmas shopping and his little sister on the back seat when a large truck had lost control of its steering and ploughed through his small car, slicing it in two. Rob had been killed instantly and his sister's legs had been ripped off.

'I wish you'd said something before,' Marnie had told her. 'You should have let me try to comfort you.'

At this she sobbed into his arms like a child. As the clock struck twelve, and even in this deserted part of the world you could hear odd distant whoops and shouts of hope for the new year and good riddance to the old, Marnie tucked her into his bed. He sat with Cathy until she fell asleep, then he climbed in beside her. Two days later she flew home for the funeral. She never came back. Marnie wrote once to see if she was all right, but no reply came. A week later a doctor confirmed that she had given him gonorrhoea.

'Poor you,' Nell said. 'It sounds awful.'

'It was pretty bad, I have to say.'

Marnie took her hand and let it go almost immediately. They finished their cups of tea and he ordered another. 'Nell,' he took her hand again, 'look I know it's ridiculously early to say so, after a few days, but I've never felt like this before about anyone, and, you know, I'm quite old.'

The waitress returned with the tea. She lingered at their table, wiping down the brown formica top and refilling the sugar bowl with little blue and white packets of sugar, each bag bearing a little saying relating to its contents, such as 'True sweetness is a boon to the world's affairs.' She took away their ashtray and brought them a clean one.

Nell sighed. 'I don't know what to say,' she said. 'I can't believe how happy it makes me when you say things like that. I mean, this kind of thing is all so completely new to me, and I feel a bit like a tourist in a completely foreign country, but I'm really really loving it.'

Marnie beamed and leaned in towards her. 'I'm so proud of you my love,' he said. 'So proud.'

Marnie left Nell in the library while he went off to keep an appointment nearby. They met again at five for some tea and toast in a different café, where they were served by an old-fashioned-looking waitress, who must have been seventy. 'This is where the ladies of the night come for four o'clock lunches,' Marnie whispered and there were one or two women, skin at once grey and rosy, sitting at the rear tables, who might have fallen into this category. Marnie was tired. Their eating of toast and drinking of tea had a nursery feel to it. After a few minutes a man who appeared to know Marnie entered the café and, without asking, came and sat at their table and embarked on a series of quick-fire questions. Was Marnie pleased with the appointment of the new poetry professor? Had he really been a safer bet than the runner-up? Marnie was patient and explained why he believed this to be the case.

Did Marnie have any thoughts on that biography of the poet, the one who was famous for being grumpy, whom they had all knocked about with in the old days?

'It was too nervously written,' Marnie said. 'I actually thought it was a bit shabby. It made me think of a man I used to know who felt he ought to be ashamed of his wife in public, and although he was really very fond of her, he was always putting her down, walked a couple of paces behind her and so on, in order to protect his own reputation.'

'Ah, he won't be pleased to hear you say that.'

Marnie shrugged his shoulders.

'And what sort of difference do you think the new editor of the City review will make. I mean, can you imagine large-scale changes?'

'I very much doubt that. Look,' Marnie said, 'I don't mean to be rude, but I'm trying to have a cup of tea with Nell here, whom I haven't seen since lunchtime, which, by the way, feels like an eternity, and I would really like a bit of peace.'

'So sorry, I quite understand,' the man said. 'One last thing, though. Did you see that essay by the

American chap in last month's *Keats and Shelley Journal* that claimed . . . ' but when the man looked up and saw Marnie's glowering eyes, he swiftly made his goodbyes and, to Marnie's great annoyance, settled their bill (£1.84) without letting on.

'I can't take him at all seriously, with that head of his lolling about like a great noodle,' he told Nell on leaving.

The more time Nell spent with Marnie, the more she minded these random people accosting him, draining and fingering him and generally treating him like public property. It was important to her that her vast interest in him, her liking, her love for him (she had not told him this yet) was entirely distinct from that of the people who bothered him all the time. Just because he made himself accessible to people, they shouldn't take advantage, asking him complex questions that were important to him in order to arouse his interest and then not even bothering to listen to his replies. Sometimes she wished he was a bit less generous in this way, that he could see immediately who his real friends were and not be taken in by hangers-on who shamelessly pumped him for information and judgements and drinks.

Marnie was quite a different character in London. For one thing he was more social; he made frequent, nervous sallies into the West End at night, 'sprees', he called them, which involved chatting to strangers (chiefly girls), smoking vast amounts of cigarettes (once seventy in one day), drinking, eating in restaurants and permanently jigging about in response to the dizzying array of choices, all the various forms of entertainment on offer to him. If a good discussion developed, he'd be happy to stay up half the night talking and drinking.

Life in college presented considerably less to contend with in this line and his time there was quieter and more serious. There were occasionally freakish and unexpected academic, social gatherings of interest within the university, but these were so rare as to be almost apocryphal. If you had an unconventional line of business, if you were a butler, for example, there was said to be great high jinks to be had at the lounge bar below one of England's remaining buttling schools, in the early hours of the morning. Marnie knew a man who taught there and he'd once been invited to a party attended entirely by trainee and qualified butlers, whose rapid consumption of an entire case of late bottled port did not compromise a single ounce of their collective, glassy *sang-froid*.

London, as far as Marnie was concerned could be relied on for adventures. Coming off the motorway and speeding up Holland Park Avenue, in the rattling sky-blue diesel Ford Fiesta, late at night which was the only time Marnie liked to drive, as they drew level with a dodgy-looking gilded French restaurant, Marnie would say to Nell, 'I do love London.' At this point he would switch on the radio and they would both attempt to join in with the random and unfamiliar pop songs that blared out, Marnie banging his fists on the steering wheel and drumming his fingers on the dashboard and Nell doing backing vocals all the way up Bayswater Road and Oxford Street until they reached his flat in Holborn.

Marnie's flat was immediately recognizable as the part-time residence of a single man. It was just three rooms on the third floor of a narrow town house: a bedroom, a light, south-facing sitting room, with a drop-leaf mahogany table, an old two-seater sofa, a desk and two odd armchairs and many, many books, and then there was a tiny galley kitchen with two electric rings, a small oven, and an array of brightly coloured enamel saucepans, hung on the wall in descending sizes. The bathroom, chiefly remarkable for the enormous and menacing cracks that covered the ceiling and extended down one wall, was shared with the man in the flat above and the woman who lived downstairs.

In the first ten days of their romance, Marnie frequently complained that he was having trouble with his work. He'd written three lines for the beginning of the new poem, but didn't seem to be getting anywhere, although he kept on writing them out over and over again. Nell wondered if he was hoping to make a mistake and write them down differently, somehow better, as perhaps a word or phrase would come to him, without the decision to think it having been reached. The lines as they stood, he said to Nell without showing them to her, were 'too expensive-sounding'.

'Do you mean, sort of deliberate without quite sounding specific?' she asked.

'That's exactly what I mean. Thank you for putting it so well.' He gave her a long look. 'So-oo hard to work with you here being so disarming.'

'I'm sorry.'

Marnie came over to where she was lying. Nell had been reading in the bedroom, lying on her front, book propped against the pillow, knees bent back against herself and feet crossed at the ankles. She had remained like this, quiet as a mouse, for the past three hours, until he had come in and asked her if she would like some tea.

'Everything's completely changed,' he said to her.

'Oh?' she said to him.

He laughed at her anxious tone. 'It's all immeasurably better,' he carried on.

'Oh good,' she said. 'Anything in particular, or just sort of generally?'

'Because of you.'

Nell scrambled to her feet to meet his comments formally. He looked her squarely in the face and her eyes closed. His arms circled her waist and he kissed her eyelids and then her nose and then she kissed his mouth as hard as she could and buried her face in his shoulder. 'I'm so impressed by you,' Marnie was confiding into her ear. 'The things you say and do. The way you go about things.'

'Don't,' Nell said, but Marnie carried on.

'I mean, when I think about the people I've been with before I just think, what did I think I was doing?' Marnie stroked her cheek, which by this time was hot with tears. 'Do you mind my talking like this?' he asked.

'No,' she said, 'I completely love it.'

They went to the kitchen to make some tea but there wasn't any milk. 'Perhaps I'll go and get some,' Nell said. Marnie sat down again in his chair. It was three and neither of them had been out all day.

'Whatever you like.'

'I could get a few other things as well.'

'Fine. Can I just give you a very quick kiss?' he asked.

'Of course.' Nell went over to him shyly and stopped about a yard from where he was sitting and waited for him to do something. She lifted her eyes from the ground to look at his face. She stood there, hovering. 'They're so lovely, your hesitancies,' he said and stood up to kiss her. Finally they disentangled their arms and Nell smiled and moved towards the door, slipping into her coat and taking her purse out of her bag. Marnie gave her a five-pound note for the shopping but Nell refused it. She opened her purse to make sure she had enough money, and found that she had about seven pounds, along with several chewed-up pieces of paper, a bus ticket, an old sweet wrapper, and a piece of card from her college doctor with the date and time of her appointment to see the counsellor written on it. Nell scrunched these pieces of paper into a ball and threw it into Marnie's waste paper bin. 'Don't be long will you?' Marnie said. 'Things seem so monochrome when you're not here.'

That night in bed he told Nell, 'Sometimes I think that what I would like to do more than anything is to draw up a table of all the things I understand and all

164

the things I don't understand and shape it so that it seems very exact and well-finished, but for it to have a feeling of having been made with completely unrestricted freedom, with a kind of irresponsibility.'

'And would it be a poem, this piece of work?'

'I think it would have to be, don't you?'

(To Nell's mind this was pillow talk of the highest calibre.) 'Really an epic poem, then?'

'In some ways, yes, although not in others.'

'Do you have a sort of fixed point where you would start, or is it too early to say?'

'No, I don't really, except I don't want it to be random or miscellaneous in any way.'

'Pretty robust, then?'

'That's it, yes. I've been thinking about it slowly for some time, but I need to think about it quickly for a bit, because it makes the thoughts different. It'll be very long, I think. A manuscript to be carried round in a suitcase. I'm gathering material for it at the moment.' He paused and looked at her.

'At this very moment?' Nell asked, feeling his hand on her breast.

'Wait and see,' Marnie answered her with a kiss on the forehead. 'Wait and see.'

Nell had not known much in the way of romance before Marnie. There was a boy, Ned, a friend of Laura's brother, who had taken a bit of a shine to her, but it was hard to take him seriously, as he was filled with such funny ideas about girls, talking about them as if they were creatures from some quite different

165

planet, full of dark mysteries and practising strange rites. His instincts, for instance, told him that girls needed constant buttering up, but he was at a loss as to know how to go about this. As a result, he swerved recklessly between a grating, strained courtliness:

Ned: Tell me, what have people said about your eyes?

Nell: Oh, Ned, Pleeeeeease.

Nell: (again) Actually my optician says I have exceptionally poor sight for someone of my age.

Ned: But you don't wear glasses?

Nell: Contact lenses.

Ned: Really, Hard or soft?

and a bizarre, saloon-bar bravado:

Nell: God, I'm tired.

Ned: What say we drive home and I help you unwind. (Long look)

Nell: (speechless)

Nell: (recovered) You came on your bike, Ned.

So, two long kisses and one night spent under the same duvet in parallel lines (and trousers) were all the preparation Nell had for her fully fledged grown-up love affair (it was an affair because he was her teacher) with Bill Marnie.

Marnie was madly in love with her. He told her on waking, whispering it into her eyes as he stroked her hair while they waited for the Teasmaid to come to the boil. Sometimes, while she was sleeping (if they were in London) he would pop out to a local bakery, where they sold hot rolls and would have the table all laid out for breakfast, with the *Financial Times* as a tablecloth and his mother's linen napkins all ready for when she awoke.

'I'm not sure of the wisdom of saying these things to you but I feel, the thing is, what I feel is that I want to be with you for ever,' he told her one morning.

Nell closed her eyes and an enormous smile that had its roots in her heart of hearts, spread across her face. 'I love you,' she answered him.

Chapter 9

One night when their romance was in its third week, Nell was out on the town with Marnie, who had described himself as in the mood for a spree. They were in a taxi en route for a small bar in Mayfair. Nell asked him what the people there would be like. 'Pretty rough, I'm afraid,' Marnie said. 'Strays, tearaways, assorted druggy youths, fast girls, sort of attractive blonde women, but with dodgy lumps and smears of oil paint on their forearms, maudlin actors, social people who write a bit, poignant drunks . . . I could go on.'

'I think I get the idea,' Nell said.

When they arrived, a pink-faced receptionist with mayonnaise-coloured hair welcomed them. 'Hi Marnie, long time no see,' she said. 'What's new and different?'

Marnie smiled and nodded but said nothing.

The room itself was so crowded and smoky that it was quite hard to breathe. Marnie seemed to be flourishing in this sort of environment and Nell felt excitable. It was the first time he had taken her to a place where people he knew would see them together, apart from to the library or one of the cafés near it, and these places were more neutral and certainly less social. Nell surveyed the room. Marnie had neglected to point out that everyone was extremely good-looking. His hand gripped hers tightly as he scanned the randomly assembled persons for familiar faces, taking the measure of the company.

Marnie seemed to command a certain respect in this setting. She was also conscious that people were looking at them. It did not seem unusual for a man in his forties to be with a nineteen-year-old girl in such a place, nevertheless there was something about the two of them, together, that Nell felt people found remarkable. Nell was aware that something in her was jigging about in anticipation, just as she noticed Marnie's head dipping and peering, eyes darting with rapid abrupt movements, mouth smiling in recognition. After a few moments, Nell attempted to prize her hand from Marnie's in order to go to the bar to get drinks and as she did so he turned to her, his face contorted with shock and fear that she no longer wanted to exist at the end of his fingers. Nell was enormously touched by this. She stayed with him, his fingers wrapped in hers for some time, he lit a cigarette, took up her hand again and then finally he let her go for a moment.

As she ordered his scotch and got one for herself too she saw him greet and strike up a conversation with an attractive, dark-haired man in his twenties. Nell looked hard at Marnie. There were two ways of looking at

Marnie. There was the man she had seen at the poetry reading in her school uniform, her nerves churning violently in her stomach and the moment constantly hammering at her, forcing her to accept the exceptional importance to her of the look of him, the sound of him. This was accompanied by the fierce wish to talk to him, to prolong their meeting at all costs, and this feeling pressed up against her, sharp and hard, reducing her to speechlessness or tears at the recognition that he really was a prince among men. The facts of him were these: he was so beautiful, so intensely clever and really he was everything it might occur to a person to long for in another person.

The other way to look at him . . . it escaped her at the moment what the other way was, but she dimly knew it was near the opposite of this way, something she guessed other girls experienced when they reckoned him up and saw in him the allure of more worldly things. Returning with the drinks, Nell caught the end of Marnie's conversation with the handsome youth. He was giving the younger man good-natured, mildly severe advice about writing, about girls. 'I mean with women,' the younger man was saying, 'I mean it's like writing, isn't it? You've got the paper and the pen and you've got to make something happen . . . '

'That's tripe, Angus,' Marnie said.

'I suppose you're right.' Then the man, with the slightly unsavoury air of a procurer, introduced Marnie to a friend of his, a small, chubby blonde girl with large eyes that looked like they might burst into tears at any minute. Nell joined them. 'Hello,' she said with a note of archness in her voice. The small girl already had Marnie's ear and his eyes had stopped darting about across the room and something in his face seemed to be flickering dimly, gradually lighting up, now almost glowing as the girl talked nineteen to the dozen. Nell stood dully on Marnie's other side.

'I know I'm standing here talking to you casually, but I mean, my God, this is such an enormous thing for me. I mean, I can't believe I'm actually standing here talking to you. It's unbelievable because I was only reading about you this afternoon. I can't tell you how much this means to me. You're my absolute hero.'

'I think I'm going to be sick,' Nell said to the girl's friend and immediately wished she hadn't.

'I do think Ruth has a bit of a crush on Marnie,' he said smilingly.

'I know,' Nell told him. 'And actually I think it's a bit tawdry.'

Then, suddenly, Marnie was suggesting that the four of them should have dinner together and they were all leaving the club in a taxi for Soho. The girl gushed on and the young man seemed to be hanging on Marnie's every word. Once seated in the discreet dining room of an Italian restaurant Nell felt that if she had to eat a single morsel of food it would get stuck in her throat. She scanned the menu for something that didn't make her feel ill. 'You choose for me?' she said to Marnie. He nodded and smiled at her. Nell went to the ladies' and sat on the pink toilet seat and burst into tears. There was a phone in the toilets and she rang Laura who was out and then she rang her mother, but there was no reply. Nell wiped her eyes, left the restaurant, jumped on a bus and made her way to her mother's house.

'You can't fucking treat people like that,' Nell said to herself on the top of the bus. She felt her face and arms colouring with the humiliation. She gave herself three sharp knocks on the side of the head and then cringed at the possibility that one of her fellow passengers might have seen. One minute he was holding on to her as if she had been valuable to him and precious and the next she had been completely replaced. She struck her head again, this time only once and prayed that no one had seen her. 'Don't do that,' she said, tears running down her face. 'Please don't do that.' She was utterly mortified now; she shrank into herself, and sat, clenched together, a ball of shame. The bus reached her stop. She tried to banish the picture of Marnie and the blonde girl from her head. But they were entwined in each other's arms and kissing and kissing and Marnie was telling her he loved her. Nell felt like she was going mad. She opened the front door of her mother's house, called out for her mother, and when there was no reply went into the kitchen and sat on the kitchen table as she had done when she was a child. Her head was aching fiercely but the warmth of the room and its familiarity soothed her. She tried to think calmly. What had Marnie actually done? He had spoken warmly to, and invited out, another girl and her friend, possibly her boyfriend. It was thoughtlessness rather than malice or rejection.

She had over-reacted wildly. She scribbled a note to her mother, 'Dropped in for ten minutes, sorry to have missed you, hope all's well at your end, have struck up a grand romance! Love Nell.' Then she washed her face, combed her hair with her mother's comb and left the house to find a taxi. In fourteen minutes' time she was back in the restaurant, all in all she had been gone for forty-five minutes.

Marnie had ordered her a plate of saffron risotto. 'I thought it would be nice and light if you were feeling a bit delicate,' he said. He was on his best behaviour. He looked at her carefully. 'Are you feeling very low?' he asked, whispering, taking her hand.

'I was, but I'm all right now.' She was close to tears and her head was spinning. She looked at the dish of food in front of her and tried to eat a few mouthfuls. The rice didn't seem to want to stay in her mouth.

'I'll take you home, my love. I'm sorry you're not feeling well but I'm so glad you came back.' Marnie fished some notes out of his wallet, tucked them under his plate, made their excuses to the young couple and soon she was fast asleep in his arms in the cab and then lying next to him in bed.

'Goodnight, my sweet precious angel,' Marnie said. 'You must realize that you're everything to me, Nell.'

'No, no,' she whispered. 'I'm nothing. Really, nothing at all.'

Then without quite knowing why she felt hot tears quickly dripping down her face and then she was sobbing and sobbing so that her whole body was heaving up and down and the pillow was sodden and she could barely catch her breath. Marnie wrapped her in his arms.

'I can't. I can't. I can't,' Nell was saying over and over again, her back hunched over and her chin digging hard into her chest.

'Talk to me, Nell,' Marnie said. 'Tell me. I've got all the time in the world for you.' He released one of her hands and started stroking her forehead. Nell was beginning to collect herself. 'I think I've been realizing a few things,' she said. 'From when I was a little girl.'

Marnie nodded. She had spoken to him about it before once or twice.

'I suppose it's just dawned on me. I don't think – I somehow feel that no one has ever, you know, I've never really been . . . I just thought I wasn't the kind of person, that well my parents, my father . . . I just never really . . . I never was, he made me feel, I mean, I let myself be . . . '

'Do you think it could be the fact of my loving you now, being very deeply, very much in love with you and here and always loving you for as long as you want it, do you think it brings it home to you that you missed, that your parents, that your father . . . '

Tact forbade him to go any further. Nell nodded, eyes closed. She began to cry again, gently at first, just with her eyes, and then it gained momentum, her whole body seemed full of sobs. 'God, I'm so sorry,' she said, trying to collect herself. 'I don't know why I'm crying when I'm so happy. Look at me, I'm so embarrassed.'

'Absolutely not,' Marnie said. 'It is something well worth crying for, my darling. I'm not in the least happy that you're sad, that you've had these losses, but if I can help you to open up about it, then I'm glad and I'm honoured. I admire your courage. Those great sobs of yours show how big your soul is. I wish I could cry like you.'

Nell kissed him. 'You really are a prince.' Marnie smiled. They were both quiet for a minute and then, 'The thing is,' Nell said, 'I think I'm completely furious.'

'Of course you are.'

'I feel like kicking him in the teeth. How could he be so mean to a little girl?'

'Well, we can't really know that,' Marnie said. 'I expect no one took much notice of him when he was a child.'

'It's no excuse.' Nell spoke the words gently, but through gritted teeth. She shook her head from side to side. 'It's no excuse.'

Marnie sighed. 'No,' he said, 'it's not an excuse, but it is an explanation. What you have to remember is that people don't do these things on purpose. People are used to the idea that their actions have consequences, but they forget that their failure to act can have an effect too.'

Next morning they were both extremely careful of each other.

Then, after only half an hour of working Marnie went into the bedroom and made a series of phone calls. Nell, puzzled, read absently until he reappeared.

'Look,' he said, 'I can't work. I feel bad about last night. I'm not quite sure what happened—'

'Please don't feel bad. It's completely fine. I'm so embarrassed about the whole thing.'

'Anyway, what would you say to going to France for the weekend?'

'What, this weekend?'

'We need a break, Nell. I could work a bit and we could swim and read and generally get back to normal.'

'I'd love to, but I mean, won't it be really expensive?'

'Yes, but I'm rather well off at the moment and there's this lovely place near Nice up a little mountain and the food's really good and one can lie by the pool and people bring you delicious things to drink. I think, unless you feel very strongly that you can't face it, we ought to go. I've asked the travel agent to arrange everything. It would be easy to cancel but—'

'I'd love to be there with you.'

At the airport Nell watched Marnie trying to grapple with things quite beyond him, finding the right queue, collecting their tickets, being polite to an air hostess who was misunderstanding him, worrying that they would miss their plane when there were seventy minutes before their flight was due to leave and her heart brimmed with pride that this great, beautiful man in his eccentric-looking holiday clothing, white crumpled shirt, pale corduroy trousers and old herring-bone coat with torn bits of lining hanging below the hem, was hers. When everything was arranged, Nell darted into a shop and bought herself a striped swimsuit (her suit being in her college room) with money Marnie gave her for the purpose. They met up at the airport bar, where Marnie was drinking whisky although it was not quite noon.

'Do you think that's a good idea?' she asked him gently. 'It's just that it might make you feel a bit low on the plane.'

'You're right, but I hate flying, it makes me really edgy. This is the only way I'll get myself on the plane.'

'But if you hate flying . . . ?' Nell's voice trailed off.

'It'll be worth it in the end. Come here,' Marnie said although she was standing right by him. She closed her eyes and took his whisky kiss on her lips.

Marnie remained as white as a sheet during the journey, bracing himself against the edge of his seat. To ease his suffering Nell tried to distract him with kisses and a quiz in the magazine she had found on her seat.

Your partner is away on business for the weekend. Do you:
a. Use the time to do all those household chores you've been putting off, and to catch up with old friends
b. Call up your ex and suggest dinner and a movie
c. Phone him or her at regular intervals because you suspect foul play

But when Nell turned to Marnie for his answer he was asleep.

from: Le Soleil d'Or, St Paul de Vence, FRANCE
Dear Laura,
I knew the South of France was quite a place, but I didn't realize it was such an enormous deal. There are some very bad

taste people here, men all stomach and no hair accompanied by women (generally other people's wives) with two feet of golden tresses and six inches of black roots, dressed in clingy white mini dresses with diamante trim and little mink tassels and baby pink appliquéd parrot motifs AT BREAK-FAST. Then there are the good taste people, discreet well-dressed men, mainly art collectors, it seems, in their early fifties with twenty-five-year-old serious convent-educated international beauty wives called Jennifer or Helen. And me and Marnie. He seems very relaxed here, eating and swimming, not drinking too much (I think because he knows I worry about it a bit) and he's even managed to stop thinking about work for a second. Simone Signoret and Yves Montand had their honeymoon here apparently. It's a bit cold at this time of year but there's a beautiful dining room outside overhung with fig leaves and we eat simple food of the highest quality, cooked plainly with a glass or two of rosé.

I suppose the big news is that he's asked me to marry him. AFTER THREE WEEKS. I have to tell you I am seriously considering it, although of course blah blah early days blah blah. He was married once before, only for three years, when he was twenty-three, but it all went horribly wrong. (Her fault – she left him.) I think it's really touching him being married so young. Anyway, I told him to ask me again in six months and he was completely fine about it.

Loll, I know I'm really flying high now and last time we met I was in the depths of despair. I wanted to write sooner and thank you for all your support. I was absolutely desperate and I feel embarrassed about it and anxious that you or I or someone might think that this is all too good to be true, and

*perhaps it is. But all I know is I've never been happier in my
life and it doesn't seem a hysterical thing. It feels quite calm.
We go for lots of walks and Marnie says things like, 'I know
you absolutely don't need it but I want to protect and help you
and make your life easier.' Isn't that lovely? You see it all feels
so strong and real. To be properly loved by someone, and by
someone who's made of such fine stuff. It really does feel like a
miracle. Some of the things he says are so clever it practically
hurts my brain to try and process them. I'm not completely sure
what he sees in me, but I know it's a lot. I feel very sure of him.
He has got a great mind in a grand sort of way, but he hasn't
got his head in the clouds at all. He stroked my stomach for
about an hour last night when I had a bad pain. I really
respect him, what he's trying to do, the way he leads his life
and so on and then he's so handsome. Sometimes I'm too
embarrassed to look at him. I'm sure people will think he's
only after one thing but if anything it's the other way round.
It's not as if I'm some starry-eyed little girl and he's this great
man, because he does love me really properly. He's always
asking my opinion about things and trying things out on me.
He's made my life so nice. I'm so happy. I'll probably be home
by the time you get this. I can't wait to see you.*

    All my love, Nell.

Just as she put down the pen Marnie returned from
taking a swim. In his white towelling dressing gown he
looked alarmingly frail and spindly to Nell, almost like
an old man. He seemed to be moving stiffly. 'Are you all
right there?' she asked him, sidling up to where he was
standing near their bed and taking his hand. Marnie

sat down on the bed with its yellow gingham cover. He was still wet from the swimming pool and his hair dripped little tears down his face. Nell stroked his hand. 'Feeling a bit low?' she whispered. Marnie buried his head into her shoulder and Nell wrapped her arms round him. He was shaking gently and when Nell leaned down and peered up at the face he was hiding from her she could see that it wasn't just his hair that was dripping onto his face, he was crying real tears. 'What's the matter, darling? Can you tell me?' And then suddenly it seemed unbearable to her that he should be feeling so unhappy in her company that he needed to cry and she began to cry too. 'Oh dear,' Marnie said. Nell nodded in agreement. 'I love you Nell. Whatever happens. I do love you.'

'What do you mean, whatever happens?' she asked. 'Nothing's going to happen. I hate that kind of talk.'

'You're right,' Marnie said, as always. 'I'm sorry. I'm just weak and cowardly.'

'You're not. That's rubbish.'

Marnie held her close to him. 'I'm so impressed by you,' he said. 'Your good sense and your beauty and your cheerfulness.'

'No,' Nell said. 'No.' She shook her head. 'All this is more than I could ever have hoped for. I mean I did hope for it, I hoped for it for weeks before anything happened at all, but . . . Oh, you know what I mean.'

Marnie nodded. 'It's really really strong,' he said and more tears rolled down his cheek.

'Now what can we do to cheer you up?' Nell said.

'I could think of something.' Nell raised her eyebrows at him and he pulled her back onto the bed. 'I wish I could make love to you properly,' he said. Up till now their love-making had stopped short of intercourse at Nell's request.

Nell didn't say anything.

'Nell?'

'I'm just thinking.'

'Talk to me about it.'

But Nell didn't talk, she just planted a large kiss on Marnie's lips and began taking off her clothes.

'Are you sure?' he asked her.

She nodded.

They both got into bed and Marnie began stroking her arms and legs and kissing her neck and her ears and the back of her knees and her forehead and her hip bones which at other times he called 'razor sharp'.

It was three o'clock in the afternoon. Bright French sunlight poured through the three long windows which gave on to their balcony where the remains of their lunch lay on a wooden tray. Nell was breathing heavily, her eyes were closed and she felt tiny, dwarfed by the enormity of the desire she was feeling. Marnie was stroking her forehead with one hand as if to calm down a feverish child and with the other hand he was tickling her between the legs. Nell swivelled her hips round and his finger reached into her vagina. ('Are you sure my darling?' 'Never been surer.') His penis followed.

The day after they returned from France, Marnie

announced that a friend of his, Noel, and his wife were coming round for dinner that night. Marnie spent most of the afternoon at the shops and came home laden with a bunch of yellow roses for the table and an assortment of carrier bags, some bearing the names of long-established food shops and some red-and-white-striped bags from Berwick Street market.

'Perhaps I ought to make myself scarce,' Nell said as the hour grew nearer.

'Oh, no!'

'Well . . . I don't exactly have to but . . . '

'You must stay, then.'

'Of course I'll stay,' Nell caved in. 'Only you must let me help you. Is there anything I can chop up?'

'Absolutely not,' said Marnie, 'but you can talk to me and help yourself to a drink.' Nell obeyed. Although it was only four o'clock, it seemed the right thing to do.

'So what does Noel's wife do?'

'I don't know, really. I suppose she's a sort of poet's wife of the old school. She arranges all the aspects of his life in the way most likely to facilitate his writing.'

'Oh,' said Nell.

'When I see them together, I think of American poets in the forties and fifties when they used to rent enormous houses in the country and the women would cook and clean and write novels and the men would do the dishes after dinner, talking about Shakespeare and try to write poems in the daytime and on Saturday nights they would all get dressed up and go dancing.'

'That sounds perfect.'

'It was and it wasn't. A lot of the time they were extremely unhappy. You know that John Berryman killed himself and Delmore Schwartz died in a terrible sort of hotel, completely alone, and wasn't missed for several days and Randall Jarrell killed himself too and Lowell had a heart attack in the taxi leaving his second wife to go back to his first, or was it his third for his second.'

'No, I didn't know,' Nell said quietly. Marnie had fallen into a silent reverie.

After some time Nell asked, 'So, does Noel's wife write novels then?'

'No, she doesn't, or at least I've never heard any mention of it.'

'Do they have children?'

'No, they don't. I think she would quite like to, but Noel, I suppose he thinks it would be too disruptive.'

'And do you think she's happy with the way things are?'

'I don't know. She's immensely kind, kind almost to the point of lunacy, but I don't quite know what that indicates.'

'It's certainly not the same as being happy.'

'No.'

'What's she like, Noel's wife? What's her name?'

'She's called Judith. She's very tall and quite serious looking and intelligent,' Marnie said, 'and extremely good natured.'

'Do you think she's a bit of a victim?'

'A victim of what?'

'Of her husband's.'

'I don't think so. They love each other. She knows what she's doing.'

While Marnie nipped out to get some drink Nell cleared the table in the sitting room and placed Marnie's books and papers carefully on top of the bed, making sure to keep everything in the same order. The plates that Marnie had set to warm up on top of the stove were a little dusty and Nell gave them a good rinse under the hot tap, searching in several drawers until she found a dish cloth with which to dry them. In the drawer she also saw a tablecloth and she dragged the iron and ironing board from the cupboard by the front door and as the cloth was dry and heavily creased, Nell wetted her hand several times under the cold tap and shook her fingers over the fabric to dampen it and make the job easier. Just as she spread the material out on the table the doorbell rang.

'Hello?' the woman said, a little flustered.

'Oh, hi, I'm Nell. Marnie's just nipped out to get something. He won't be a minute. Please come in. Will you have a drink?'

'Thank you,' the man said, following his wife into the room, and he in turn was followed by Marnie. The four of them stood together, occupying most of the space in the little sitting room. Nell slipped into the kitchen to get some glasses. Marnie only had three, so for herself she took a teacup; she liked drinking alcohol from china. Marnie's friends had brought a bottle of champagne. Noel opened it smoothly and poured it out. 'What's your favourite toast?' he asked Nell. After a moment she replied, 'Cheers!' 'Cheers' they all echoed and clicked their glasses and the old glass made a high ringing sound unlike Nell's cup, which sounded flat and curt.

Noel's wife immediately struck up conversation with Nell. 'Would you like any help with the meal?'

'Marnie's done everything.'

'Really?' The woman was taken aback. 'Don't tell me he ironed the tablecloth?'

'I did actually do that,' Nell conceded.

Marnie was offering them more wine. 'Nell?' he said. 'Judith?' Neither woman was ready for a refill. Judith was about forty-five, almost six foot, and had dark shiny shoulder-length hair and a girlish fringe. She was extremely womanly: calm, smiling, self-contained, humorous and lively. She wore a dark grey jersey over a white shirt, a knee-length grey tweed skirt, black tights and flat black shoes. Noel was an inch or two shorter than his wife. He was stood talking to Marnie in the kitchen, opening a bottle of red wine, although both men had moved onto whisky. Marnie was carving the leg of lamb. He carved four large portions, bathing each slice in the juices from the pan and adding a few roast potatoes to each plate. The remaining white spaces between meat and potato he filled with boiled cabbage. Nell brought the plates to the table, two by two. Marnie followed her with a jar of mint sauce and a jar of redcurrant jelly which he placed at the centre of the table. The two couples sat down to eat.

All night long, Noel and Marnie discussed poetry, their own and other people's. Nell and Judith just sat and listened. There was a certain amount of competitiveness to their memories and opinions.

Occasionally they finished off each other's sentences, pointing to rarer and rarer examples, choosing their words carefully. Nell was completely enthralled by what was being said, and kept trying to see if she could remember things word for word that had been spoken a few minutes ago, and therefore could hope that she might be able to remember them in the morning. At one point Noel expressed a liking for an acquaintance of theirs and Marnie responded, 'I don't know what to think of her, I mean everything she writes is so completely muddled. It's like a drawer with shoes and socks and even FEET in it.'

Nell had half a mind to say something at this point, but something held her back. She cleared the table. The men were talking about *Hamlet* now. 'There's no pudding, I'm afraid,' Marnie told them, pushing a plate of Stilton and some water biscuits into the middle of the table. Noel let out a howl. The men lit cigarettes. 'I'll make some coffee,' Nell said and slipped off into the kitchen. Marnie was not a pudding man. She looked in the cupboard above the sink. Anchovies and Marmite were pretty well the extent of his larder. But there was a large pot of blackcurrant jam and flour and sugar and some eggs and butter in the fridge. Nell took a large glass bowl from the cupboard and began rubbing fat and flour, until the mixture resembled bread crumbs.

Then she added an egg yolk and stirred the mixture with the blade of a knife until it resembled a thick paste. With her hands she rolled it into a ball. Then she pressed the pastry as thinly as she could into a cast-iron frying pan, spooned in and smoothed over half the contents of the jam jar and put the tart in the oven at gas mark 5. Fifteen minutes later, when Nell went back to the kitchen and appeared in the sitting room with her handiwork, she was met with cheers.

'Angel,' Marnie said.

'From Heaven,' Noel added.

She cut four slices from the tart and handed them round. Noel was ready for a second slice before Nell had begun her own. The men continued talking. Judith was looking anxious. 'We'll go in a moment,' Noel said, pouring more whisky for himself and Marnie. Two hours later they were still there. Judith was visibly annoyed. 'We must be going,' Noel would say at intervals, but he just could not tear himself away. Judith was trying to catch her husband's eye. 'I've got an interview in the morning at half past nine,' she confided to Nell. 'It's just a part-time thing, but you know . . . '

'You want to be fresh,' Nell said.

'What time is it, anyway?'

Nell went into the bedroom to look at the clock. 'Oh dear, it's actually ten to three.'

Nell went and got Noel and Judith's coats. Noel looked a little taken aback but made no complaint. Marnie began collecting up the coffee cups and they all said their goodbyes. When his friends had left Marnie asked her, calmly, what she meant by throwing his friends out of the house. 'It's half past three. Judith was exhausted and she has an interview in the morning.'

'Oh, I see. Funny she didn't mention it. I'm sorry darling. You were quite right.'

Despite the late hour the two of them had one last drink together.

'You know, you still haven't given me an answer, my love,' Marnie said, his arm stroking Nell's stockinged foot up and down, up and down, as they lay head to toe on the sofa. He kissed her instep.

'I know I haven't,' Nell answered him. 'I want you to ask me again in three months. I'm almost completely certain though,' Nell said. 'I just need to be a bit surer of things. I don't mean things to do with you, I mean things to do with me.'

'What sort of things?'

'Well, I'd hate to do anything for the wrong reasons.'

'What would the wrong reasons be?'

'Well, I suppose marrying you just because I'm completely in love with you and I think you're the most . . . the greatest person I've ever met.'

'And those are the wrong reasons?'

'Yes. I mean no, but I need to work out things to do with me. It's maybe different for you.'

'Because of being so much older?'

'Because this kind of life is all so new.'

'It's new to you, I can see that. It's all right, my love. I can wait. I've got all the patience in the world for you. We'll wait until you're quite sure.'

'Thank you,' Nell said. She kissed him on the lips.

'I love you.'

'I love you.'

'No, no, no, no, no. I insist. I love YOU.'

'No, no, no, no, no, there's been a mistake, you've got things muddled up, you see, I love YOU.'

'You're wrong because the truth of the matter is that I love YOU.'

'No, please I insist . . . '

'This is so lovely,' Marnie said, stroking the edge of her calf. Nell was running her index finger along the line of his toes.

'I know,' Nell said. 'I'm so impressed by us. I mean, if I didn't know us and I met us I'd think, God they know how to live those people. I'd be green with envy.'

'It's true,' Marnie nodded. 'More people should be like us.'

'I quite agree. What are they thinking of, those people?'

'Which people?'

'You know, the ones who are not like us.'

'I don't really know. Evidently rather little, I should say.'

Marnie's middle finger was weaving little circles of pleasure behind Nell's left knee.

'Oooh, that's lovely,' she said.

'You're lovely,' he told her.

'You know what,' she said gathering herself up from her end of the sofa and lowering herself, as gracefully as possible, onto his side, onto him, 'I think we both are.'

Chapter 10

Then, after four weeks of bliss between the two of them, without the merest hint of a warning, Marnie sank into such a severe depression that his GP insisted on hospitalization. His descent was rapid and uncommunicated. He and Nell had parted on Monday, she had left him working in London and returned to college for a series of lectures, and he had waved her chirpily onto the train at Paddington, wearing the yellow cashmere socks she had bought him as a present. When she had telephoned him later that night he had been his usual self, but had seemed quieter than usual and complained of feeling tired. When she had phoned him the next day he had seemed a little unfocused and distracted. By Thursday, she had definitely noticed him sounding distant, but had put it down to the fact that she had spoken to him early in the morning when he had just woken, and late at night when he was already in bed. On Friday there was no reply when she rang him at regular intervals throughout the day and then on Saturday morning she had received a postcard in an unfamiliar hand, stating coolly that he had been admitted to the psychiatric ward of one of the Headford hospitals.

With the envelope in her hand, Nell ran to the high street and hailed a taxi to take her to the hospital. The cab dropped her at the entrance to the hospital, which was situated in the middle of bright green lawns edged with shrubbery and bordered by bare, thin lime trees. It was a huge set of buildings, part modern, part Victorian, with numerous separate departments and clinics. Nell raced around the brick and concrete complex, requesting information from passers-by, entering the main reception area, where there seemed to be an absence of staff, the only information available coming from a large noticeboard that bore the following message, 'Average wait for non-life-threatening cases, 3–4 hours.' Nell carried on looking, running along the corridor, stumbling randomly into different wards and nursing stations only to be given a whole new set of directions. She wove her way past oddly named signposts. 'Ear clinic' proclaimed one arrow, and adjacent to it another pointed to 'Throat and Nose' as if a body had been hacked up and the pieces variously carted off.

Finally Nell found an arrow pointing to 'The Wellesley Psychiatric Unit'. She sped along the echoing, pale yellow passageway which took her into the oldest part of the building. It was windowless but harshly illumined by a series of fluorescent lighting strips. The floors, the skirting and the occasional pieces of furniture Nell noticed were not at all clean and this, coupled with the nauseating yellowness of the walls, made her heart sink. And then, at the end of the corridor, in a dimly lit dayroom, stuck in front of a huge TV set with poor reception was Marnie, smoking, alone in a semicircle of orange plastic seats.

'Marnie!' Nell called out and as he slowly turned to face her she saw his troubled state of mind reflected in his features and it filled her with despair. He looked completely distorted, his mood seemed to have entirely altered his proportions and the man who sat before her looked all askew, his skin ill fitting, his limbs and torso misshapen and quite at a loss. His ordinarily impressive bearing had been reduced to that of a docile child, but at the same time his body seemed flabbier, larded with a new heaviness as if his bones had caved in, leaving the flesh lolling, weak and unsupported. His face barely flickered at the sight of Nell. He was beyond responding. He stood up, looking nowhere in particular for a few moments, concentrating on his smoking.

'Hello, my love,' Nell said as calmly as she could. But it seemed that Marnie could not even entertain the idea of someone else in this mood, let alone admit a real person. He took his seat again, not betraying any signs of having taken her in. Nell battled with herself and managed a smile. She went to him and took his hand. There was a soap opera on the television which Marnie seemed absorbed in, but when she looked closely it was clear that his pupils were fixed on a point inches above the screen on the blank, shiny wall. Then Nell realized he must be drugged up to the eyeballs. He stubbed out a cigarette and then loosed his hand from hers to light another one, returning his hand once the tip was safely glowing. There were no signs of any other patients or any hospital staff at all. Nell and Marnie sat in the middle of the row of seats watching the programme as if in a little cinema of their own. On screen a middle-aged couple were having a blazing row. Accusations of all sorts were flying: infidelity, jealousy, frigidity, over-spending. Their voices grew angrier and louder and shriller, until, suddenly, the man struck the woman and they both fell silent, shocked at what had occurred between them. From time to time ash fell from the end of Marnie's cigarette onto the carpet or the knee of his sky blue pyjamas.

The stillness ended abruptly with the sound of screaming. A young man, younger, Nell thought, than she was, was tearing down the corridor towards them wearing jeans and nothing else. He ran into the dayroom and sat down next to Nell. He said a breathless Hello very loudly and Nell said Hello back in a tiny voice. Marnie said nothing. There seemed nothing unusual to him in this scene. The man licked the fingers of his right hand and then slipped them under the waist band of his trousers and began to masturbate. Nell looked to Marnie for what to do, she nudged him gently so that he could see what was going on, but he did not respond, not even when she stood up, laid her hand on his shoulder and said, despairingly, 'I'd better go.' The youth called after her, 'Slaaag',

'Cuuunt.' Still Marnie said nothing. On the way out Nell passed a nurse.

'How did you get in here?' she asked. 'Visitors aren't allowed until twelve.'

'There wasn't anybody here so, I'm sorry, I just walked in.'

'Didn't you think to ring first?'

'No, I just came straight here. I didn't think . . . '

'Why not?' the nurse demanded.

'I'm sorry, I . . .'

'In future, make sure your visits coincide with hospital visiting hours. Please leave now.'

'There's a man in the TV room, um, in a bit of a state.'

'I see,' the nurse said and walked off in that direction. Nell lingered in the corridor. She could hear the nurse. 'That's enough of that,' she said tartly. 'It's dinner time now. Let's all go and wash our hands, shall we? Come on Mr Marnie, you like cottage pie.' It was eleven a.m.

Once, Marnie had told Nell, he had been so ill (she had assumed, for some reason, that it had been one of the old-fashioned illnesses that people didn't get any more and he had not corrected her assumption) that sitting on a bus he could not even tell if the people sitting all around him were men or women. And then he had forgotten things, not just past events and the names and the faces of the people he knew, but actual things, for example, he was unable to remember what a sausage was. This came as a challenge to the nurses. 'It's a long meaty thing,' they said. 'Meaty?' he said. 'There's peas as well, little green balls, savoury,

vegetable. Or there's steak and kidney pie, pastry gravy
meaty, filling, rich, hearty.'

'Hearty,' said Marnie. 'I'll have that one please.'
Leaving the hospital this anecdote came back to her. It
must have been an illness like this that he was speaking
of.

Nell took the bus back to college. She needed to speak
to someone. She thought of going to look for Robbie
until she remembered he had gone home for the
weekend and anyway she wasn't quite sure how things
stood between them. There was Helen, but she
wouldn't do. Nell went to the pay phone that was next
to the pigeon holes in the porter's lodge and telephoned
Laura, but there was no reply. She rang again and left a
message for her with the college saying, *'Ring Nell
Urgent.'* When she had put down the phone she
remembered that Laura's end of term exams started
the next day. She hadn't even sent her a card. She tried
calling her mother, but there was only the brisk
ansaphone message saying that she had gone away for
the weekend. She left a message saying, 'Please ring as
soon as you get back', then feeling that this might alarm
her mother she had added, 'It's nothing bad.' She
banged at her head with her fist. She could go and find
Sarah or Lisa or Debbie, or someone else from the
course, but she didn't know them well enough. There
wasn't anyone.

Crushed and shaking at this failure, Nell looked
absently through her pigeon hole, searching for something that might help her situation. What she did find

195

was a postcard. Nell put her hand to her head, 'That's all I need,' she said out loud. In her hands she held a message from Richard Fisher asking her to meet him for lunch the day after tomorrow in a restaurant near Trafalgar Square at two-thirty p.m. There was a number she was to dial and leave a message if she couldn't make it. The card was dated eight days earlier and had been sent from London W1. It struck Nell that it had been nearly a week since she had last checked for any mail. Laura and Marnie and her mother always left phone messages with the college and she didn't really care about anyone else.

It was three years since she had last seen him. He couldn't have picked a worse time. It would be quite impossible for her to go to London, to leave Marnie at the moment, things being as they were. She would ring the number later and say she couldn't make it. She felt a surge of dread when it hit her that she hadn't even thanked him for the thousand pounds he had sent. She and Marnie had discussed her father again recently. One day while they were having breakfast, Marnie said, 'I've been thinking over what you were saying last night, and I thought maybe it would help if you wrote down a few things about what happened when you were little. Maybe it would help you get things clearer in your head.' And Nell had done this, compiled a list of objections so that on a piece of paper stored quietly in a drawer she could feel freer of them than she could, carrying them around in her head. It seemed extraordinary to her now that only a week or so ago he was making suggestions as to how she could manage her life better.

When Nell went in to see Marnie the following day she found him lying on his bed in his pyjamas holding the hand of a male nurse, crying noisily and with much release of fluids so that his hands and face and clothes were damp and shiny. He talked between the large, hiccupping sobs, reeling off long lists of words punctuated by much coughing and wheezing and attempted catchings of breath. Nell watched from the door of the small ward and the nurse beckoned Nell to where he was standing, indicating that Nell should slip into his chair and take over. Nell took Marnie's hand in hers. Now, he was spluttering out words that appeared to torment him. Nell could only catch the meaning of an occasional word, but Marnie seemed to be viewing himself as the perpetrator of some hideous crime, and his guilt and capacity for remorse over this act were making him choke. Nell was worried that he would not be able to recover his breath. His nose had started bleeding also and drops of blood fell on his chin and down the front of his nightclothes. Nell ran into the corridor and called out, 'Nurse! Nurse!' but no one seemed to respond. She returned to the bedside and tried to understand what Marnie was saying. She wiped his nose with her handkerchief. Marnie was talking about a father and a son; he appeared to be telling a story about a mythical father and his son who had been ill-treated by the parent, or was it that the younger man had behaved badly, it was unclear. For some reason these two estranged people were seeking each other's forgiveness, were in desperate need of it, each having committed such heinous acts that they could not go on living without some sort of release. The story made no sense to Nell. It was not clear who the real criminal was. The feelings that it seemed to stir up in Marnie were extreme, though. The whole incident, the betrayal and disappointment, was causing him great anguish. Nell wondered if this was a theme he had taken up from his reading, if he hadn't sunk into a familiar model of despair where unhappiness was more easily explained in terms of ungrateful children. Then she had a thought that shocked her. She had spoken to him briefly about her own father, but surely the story could not have touched his heart to such an extent that it was playing on him mercilessly now. It was her story, after all. And yet although they had never spoken of it directly, the facts were there, that she had had a difficult relation with her own father and had ended up falling in love with a much older man, a man more than twice her age. Both of them had had an understanding that although these were some of the facts of their romance, there were many others that were subtler and more sturdy. Whatever age Marnie was, there were qualities in him which it would be impossible for Nell not to admire. Once he had praised her understanding. 'I love the way I can tell you things and you know immediately what I mean, I don't have to explain with you. You just take in what I say. I think that's really unusual in someone . . . '

'In someone of my age.' She said it flatly and quietly.

'In anyone at all. It's quite extraordinary to feel so deeply understood.'

Nell tried another tack. Could Marnie have a son that he had ill treated? Had he been betrayed by his own father? He had barely spoken of his parents over the past few weeks, apart from the scene he had painted of the couple in the bedroom anxious for his romantic wellbeing. While her mind raced through her thoughts, Nell gradually noticed that Marnie was no longer speaking of children and fathers any more, but was repeatedly using the word, 'Jack' or 'Jake'. This name rang no bells with Nell. 'Who is it, my love? Can I get someone for you? Who is it that you want, my darling? Please tell me?' Then it occurred to Nell, perhaps he was calling for Jacqueline, his ex-wife. It wasn't impossible. She steeled herself against any pang of jealousy. He had been so strong for her. She tried to ask him about the word, but Marnie had worked himself up into a great state and was waving his arms in the air, and kicking his legs up from where they lay on the bed with sudden violent jerky movements. His words were coming out thicker and faster and by this point were entirely unintelligible. Then his ranting stopped and the only sounds that came from him were choking and sobbing again.

Nell wrapped her arms around the man, but the touch of her did not console him at all. His sobs became wails; the noise was deafening and brought the nurse back. 'I'm going to give him something to settle him, he said and held his head forward, gave him a pill to swallow and a glass of water to wash it down. Nell and the nurse dragged the bed covers from under him and remade the bed over his body. Then the nurse went off to see to another patient who was calling out to him. Nell wiped Marnie's face free of blood and mucus with some wetted tissues and stayed with him until he fell asleep.

After this, she went to the hospital toilets to wash her face and hands, which were burning hot. She looked at her face in the mirror, saw it calm and unflustered. She raised her arm into the air and brought her fist down hard on her head three times. 'Everything has fallen to bits,' she said quietly, feeling the full force of the abandonment. 'What am I going to do? What am I going to do?' she asked the face in the mirror over and over again. Nell had no idea about the future except for a strong sense that she and Marnie had taken each other on and that, despite his current behaviour, perhaps even because of it, they still had this under-standing. There was no alternative. Wiping her eyes and blowing her nose she thought back to the brief conversation she had had with a nurse on her last visit.

'What's happened to him? Why has he gone like this?'

'He's had a breakdown. Could be a million reasons, love, or,' she stopped and looked thoughtfully at Nell, 'could be none.'

Nell went to visit him the next day, this time within the official visiting hours. She sat and talked with him in the room he shared with two other men, but they were alone, the men having been taken off on an outing to a nearby park. Marnie had refused to go. They both sat on low armchairs next to his bed. Marnie was much calmer today.

'Can you try and tell me what it feels like, so that I can understand?' Nell asked.

'I could try,' Marnie said. 'But words aren't very . . . ' he didn't finish. They were quiet for a bit then Nell tried again.

'Maybe you could explain it in another way.'

'Read the poems,' Marnie said.

'It's not the same, though.'

'No, you're right. It's not the same.'

'I didn't mean some public thing you'd made, to be looked at by strangers, I was thinking of anything, I don't know, a scream even, just so that things don't shut down completely between us.'

'I'm so sorry, Nell.'

'I don't mind, it's not that at all. I just want to help if I possibly can.'

'You can't. People have tried before.'

'Well, I'll just have to prove you wrong.'

But Marnie couldn't even manage a smile. Instead, with the remote control he turned up the television show that was playing quietly in the corner. Both of them looked at the screen for a few minutes.

Then Marnie spoke. 'Nell?'

'Yeah?'

'Will you take your shirt off?'

'Do you think that's a good idea?'

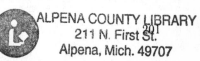

'Ah, I knew you'd say that.'

Nell got up from the chair, closed the door of the room, slipped out of her jersey and bra and lay down on the bed. It was boiling hot in the ward as it was in the hospital as a whole, but she shivered. After a short while, Marnie got up from his chair and came over to her. He stood above her, looking at her. Although her eyes were closed he must have seen that she was crying. He moved away from the bed. 'Forget it,' he said and walked out of the room. Nell put her bra and jumper back on, arranged the fruit she had bought him in the bowl on his bedside table, then pulled on her coat and gloves and left.

If Marnie was pining for Jacqueline, then perhaps she ought to be contacted, Nell told herself bravely. Life with her had been extremely complicated, it seemed. One night, prompted by an enquiry from Nell, they had discussed her in some detail.

Being with Jacqueline was like eating sweets, Marnie had told her. You thought it was the nicest thing in the world but suddenly it felt cloying, a bit bad for the health.

'What does that mean?'

'Well, everything was always so extreme for her. I think she was one of the most dishonest people I've ever met. It was really unusual for her to tell the truth. About big things she sometimes did, but about little things it was absolutely hopeless. I remember once we were walking in the park and we had to be somewhere at one and I asked a woman walking by if she had the time and she just told us, plainly, what the time was, I think she may have leaned her wrist towards me so that I could make out the numbers for myself as she told me what they were, and I remember thinking, this is absolutely extraordinary. You ask someone a question and they give you a straight answer. I know it sounds mad, but it was actually moving, this complete stranger opening up to us. That was when I knew that it was no good, Jacqueline and me, any more. She left soon after that. She's on her third husband now. Quite a famous actor. Can't remember his name. Sort of dashing, I'm sure you'd know. There's a youngish child, Sarah, I think, who's very good looking. Anyway, she writes a bit. I think with some success. You can buy them in the shops. I see her about once a year at parties. I wish her well, really.'

Nell left the ward. In the corridor the male nurse stopped to talk to her. 'I think it's going to take a while,' he said to Nell. 'He opened up a bit last night before he had his medication. He seems to have taken a bit of a shine to me for some reason. Sister said he was calling out my name this morning. We had a bit of a chat last night.'

Nell looked down at his badge through her tears and saw that the man's name was Jack Evans. It was the nurse he had been calling for. The nurse was still talking. 'You must remember that he doesn't know what he's doing. He can't really be held responsible for his actions at the moment.'

He won't talk to me, she thought.

'It must be very hard for you, I've seen cases much worse than him come right. You mustn't lose hope.'

Nell left the hospital and walked around in the grounds for a few minutes. The grass was hardened by the night before's frost. It was half past twelve. With a pang of regret she realized that she had forgotten to ring and cancel the lunch with her father. She walked out of the gates onto the pavement. She didn't know what to think about Marnie, but then it struck her that if a bus came straight away she could be in London in an hour if the traffic was good. Sometimes it made sense to jump straight out of the frying pan into the fire. As she was wondering, two London coaches did pull up and she took the second one, telling herself that going to London did not mean that she had to meet up with him. (Fisher didn't like it when people said 'met up with' she remembered. 'Met' was enough.) She could go home for the night, or catch a train to see Laura if she couldn't face him. And yet right now the meeting seemed strangely attractive.

Nell slept on the bus, waking up in the nick of time as they approached Marble Arch. The bus had been stuffy and smoky and as soon as she drew a deep breath at the bottom of Park Lane she thought how fresh the air seemed. Taking a bus up Oxford Street she arrived in Charing Cross Road with half an hour to kill, still not quite having decided if she would meet her father or not. The bookshops in the Charing Cross Road were places she and her father had enjoyed browsing in when she was eleven and twelve. She had half an idea what she was looking for. An elderly man was seated behind a desk at the rear of the first shop she came to, sipping from a styrofoam cup of coffee and eating a wholemeal scone. 'Can I help you at all?' he said to Nell.

'Yeah, I don't suppose you've got anything by . . . ' Nell was surprised that it was actually hard for her to say the name . . . 'by Jacqueline Browne have you? You know that woman who's marrie—'

'I know who you mean. Yeah, we often have her books in. I think one of them got remaindered. Yeah, we had one of her novels in last week. She's written two, hasn't she?'

'Yeah,' Nell said, 'I think so.'

'That's right. Yeah, there's *In the Soup* and *Hush Little Baby*. We had the second one in last week. There's a memoir as well, isn't there?'

'Is there? What, written recently?'

'Came out in 1988, I think, called, um, *Men of Iron*, yeah that's it. I see it about sometimes.'

'But you haven't got it?'

'I'm afraid not. They might well have it next door, though. They've got a lot of that sort of thing.'

'Thanks.' But the assistant next door was less well informed.

'Have a look,' he said, and waved vaguely in the direction of a huge bookshelf crammed with randomly selected volumes and labelled 'Lit. Biography/ Memoir/General Interest'. And there, immediately, Nell saw what she was looking for, a neat burgundy hardback, lacking its jacket, entitled *Men of Iron: A*

Memoir by Jacqueline Browne.

Nell took the book from the shelf and began nervously reading the information on the inside cover. She stopped for a moment. It seemed a terrible way to find out about someone, almost deceitful, like reading someone else's letters. Marnie had not mentioned the memoir.

Jacqueline Browne, it said, the wife of the successful film actor, had written a witty and concentrated account of her life with ——, had catalogued the eccentricities of their dazzling circle of friends, generously revealed all their best theatrical anecdotes and outlined her view of what exactly an actor's wife's role was. There was no mention, Nell was partly relieved and partly disappointed, of the fact that between eighteen and twenty-two Jacqueline had been married to poet and critic, Bill Marnie.

Nell opened the book at the contents page and read.

CONTENTS.

Nell turned over pages rapidly until she found what she was looking for. There was his name in the very first line of chapter three.

The first time I met Bill Marnie he took my breath away. I have felt deep love in my time and I've had my share of grand passions, but never has a perfect stranger knocked the stuffing out of me like that. I cried that night because I knew my life would never be the same again. I felt sick. I couldn't sleep, I couldn't eat, but I was seventeen and it seemed to me the most wonderful thing in the world. So when he asked me to marry him, there was no trace of hesitation in my voice when I said YES.

Of course everyone tried to talk me out of it. When I told father that Marnie was a poet, he nearly hit the roof. He thought they were all no-good, penniless adulterers. Mother said I should have a long engagement. Even Marnie's family tried to persuade us to wait. Once Marnie became so angry at something his sister said to us on the subject that he started shaking, turned white and passed out. His sister just stood over him stroking his brow and asking, 'What kind of marriage are you going to have if he keels over every time you have a row?'

'We never have rows,' I said proudly.

It was then that she told me about Marnie's history of mental problems. It had started when he was eighteen. She had come home one day to find him lying on the floor and howling like an animal, kicking his legs and scratching at the floorboards. Another time he'd locked himself in his room for two weeks and they'd had to call the fire brigade to get him out. The room stank and Marnie lay shrivelled in the corner, crying his eyes out. Then when he was twenty he'd been admitted to hospital for depression. They thought I lacked the staying power to handle their darling if the bad times came back. (He'd been all right for almost two years when I met him.) 'How will you cope if he goes down again,' she asked me.

I suppose I was a fool but I truly believed that love would cure him. 'I'll cope,' I said. 'I'll cope.'

I didn't have a clue. The first time Marnie got ill he treated me like a stranger. He was totally transformed from the man I had fallen for. There was no warmth, no affection, no conversation at all, nothing, and me? Well I was an unholy mess of pity, anger and guilt. The guilt was the hardest part because try as I might, and Lord knows I did try, I just couldn't love him when he was like that, ignoring me for days on end, acting like I was disgusting to him, not coming anywhere near me. I was all churned up with guilt, but I wouldn't admit defeat. I had never failed at anything in my life and I wasn't about to start. My marriage was going to be a great success, I told myself. We just needed more time. I nearly killed myself trying to understand him, making allowances, opening up to him when he came through the bad times, earning his trust, proving how reliable and kind I could be.

After three years I realized my own health was suffering. I had had a miscarriage and was drinking too much; the doctor told me I had to leave him. At first I said, 'That's quite impossible.' I'd married him for better or worse, in sickness and in health, and that was that. Marnie was always a very brave man. Even when he was very ill he still carried on teaching, dragging himself up from the blackest mood, life between his teeth, going in to college in a taxi to hold forth about a book he was crazy about, when only an hour before he had been lying under two blankets as well as our winter coats (he did feel the cold terribly) or crying in the office of his shrink. I still meet people to this day who have never forgotten what an inspired teacher he was, so it was obviously worth it. Instead, I took a two-week holiday with my mother and father and arranged for his sister to come and stay in the flat instead. During my absence Marnie started carrying on with one of his students, and that was the final straw. His sister remained in the flat and I moved all my things out one afternoon while he was at the university.

About a year later, when I had just about picked up the pieces of my life, Marnie tried to win me back. He wrote to me from hospital. He'd drawn up a new marriage contract for us, one that took into account his difficulties and my feelings. It involved the employment of a live-in nurse for six months of the year, and we would rent the studio flat upstairs where he and the nurse would live when he was ill so I wasn't disturbed. When each period of illness passed he would move back into the flat. We would pay for the flat with the money he would save from giving up cigarettes and drinking and with the money that came from the extra journalism work he was hoping to get. In this way his illness would not affect me so much, he wrote. Well, of course, this was out of the question and I wrote and told him so. He accepted my decision, saying that he had complete respect for my views on the subject. He hoped I would find some kind of happiness again. He was worried, of course, that he had broken me in some way, done some terrible damage by giving me so much to manage so young. When I remarried five years later and when my first daughter was born he sent me a telegram, warmly congratulating me, and I remember thinking that part of this goodwill must have come from his intense relief at the proof that he had not ruined my life.

Nell banged the book shut, paid for it at the counter and went off to meet her father.

Chapter 11

By the time Nell arrived at the restaurant, she was feeling so confused that she couldn't even think what she had come for. The morning's events were just beginning to hit her. Marnie's utter despair, his rejection of her breasts, Jacqueline Browne's gossipy memoir. What any of these things said about her future she did not know. She paused for a few moments at the entrance to the restaurant's bar, trying to regulate her breathing as she leaned against the cold glass. And now her father.

Two weekends before, at Marnie's suggestion, Nell had typed out the list of grievances against Fisher on Marnie's ancient typewriter, making a copy with carbon paper. One of these copies, she was hardly even aware of it now, lay folded inside the notebook which she carried with her everywhere she went.

1. You left me when I was a baby and did not make any contact with me for almost ten years.
2. You returned to London and lulled me into a false

sense of security by fixing up regular meetings which gave me the impression you had come back into my life for good.

3. Having set up a craving in me for regular meetings, you waltzed off again, informed me you were returning to America and left, having given me eight days' warning.

4. Not only has your attitude towards fatherhood been footling, cavalier and deeply unimaginative [she knew these words would grate on him more than the obvious ones, 'hopeless' and 'unkind'] you have spent the time you might have spent with me HELPING OTHER PEOPLE to overcome the shortcomings of their childhoods. This was a decision wholly lacking in logic and basic fellow feeling.

The bar gave onto a large cool room with carefully placed tables of pale wood and bright white walls. She had heard Marnie speak highly of it, and once he had arranged to meet a journalist there over the phone, while she had been sitting in his London kitchen, contentedly reading one of the Sunday supplements. It was only when she had put the magazine down and thought it curiously odd that she had bothered to check its cover and found that it was seven years out of date.

As soon as Nell entered the restaurant she saw the top of her father's head, his whole table bathed in light in a sunny corner at the far end of the room. Fisher was reading and taking sips from a glass of water. Nell crossed the room, tucking her hair behind her ears as she went, and came to a halt at the chair opposite Fisher. He stood to greet her, saying as he rose, 'How lovely to see you.' He kissed his daughter, pulling her sharply towards him. (He doesn't know how to be intimate or affectionate without making things sensual, Nell's mother had once told her.) Nell grinned for a split second as she felt his pull. 'It's so good to see you,' she said. But as he drew her near him, across the table, she lost her footing, and as she tried to recover balance, her weak legs dipped into an odd species of curtsey. She stumbled and collected her limbs. 'Sorry,' Fisher said. They both laughed shyly. Nell sat down. 'Will you have some wine?' her father asked her.

'Um, are you going to?'

'I'm not, but don't let that stop you.'

'I think I won't actually, thanks.'

'You look very well,' Fisher said.

Nell grinned and blushed and nodded.

'How are things going? Are you going to pass your finals with flying colours?'

'It's rather early to say. I've got two and a half years to go.'

'Oh, I thought it was sooner. Mine nearly killed me.'

'Oh, really?'

'But then you're so much more robust than I was,' he told her.

Nell had swallowed some drink down the wrong way and started coughing. After a few moments she got her breath back, but she had kicked over her bag and a copy of Auden's collected shorter poems had fallen out onto the floor. Fisher picked up the book. 'I love Auden,' he said.

Did he really think it would come as a surprise to her? He looked through the book. 'Where's the hymn to my profession?' he asked and when he had found it he started reading, prefacing the poem with, 'This is "In Memory of Sigmund Freud".'

> *he would unite*
> *The unequal moieties fractured*
> *By our own well-meaning sense of justice,*
>
> *Would restore to the larger the wit and the will*
> *The smaller possess but can only use*
> *For arid disputes, would give back to*
> *The son the mother's richness of feeling.*

Nell made sure not to meet his eye at this juncture. How could he speak so intimately without any irony? The list in her bag came back to her, but Fisher was in the middle of saying something. Nell switched off. Her father looked well, almost too well, not just distinguished, but somehow completely smooth and at ease. There was no trace of the wry or anxious English professional to him; in its place was a sort of international sheen. He actually looked a little like a politician or someone who had his own television show. She knew there was absolutely no chance of it, but it was almost possible to imagine him wearing make-up.

'I've got some important news,' Nell vaguely heard and started listening again.

'I'm coming back to England.'

Neither of them said anything for a few moments.

'Holiday?'

'No, for good.'

'Really?'

'I've been offered a job that's too good to refuse.' The waiter brought them their menus.

'In London?'

'Yes. It starts next month. So I've come over to try and fix up somewhere to live. I've got my eye on a very good house. It's about 1740, four floors, in a small terrace behind Manchester Square. Amazingly, it's one of the very few houses in the entire area that has a garden. I've had someone looking out for something for some time, as an investment, but when I found out about the job I asked him to look for something more substantial, he's got a very good eye, and then this property has just come on the market. I'm going to see it tomorrow afternoon. Why don't you come? Tell me what you think?'

Nell nodded eagerly, 'I'd really love to.'

The waiter returned and they gave their order. Scallops and sea bass for her father, scallops and squid ink risotto for Nell. Nell slipped off to the loo and positioned herself in front of the mirror and bashed herself on the head three times where her father had kissed it. She imitated her own voice. 'I'd really love to. I'd really love to.'

When she had met him for lunch when she was

fourteen and just before her sixteenth birthday, she had gone armed with a glassy resolve, a strong instinct about what would and what would not constitute appropriate behaviour between them. What she had resolved upon was to treat him severely, to be reserved, and to keep herself bound up and tightly closed off to him. When they had greeted each other on these occasions she intended to remain aloof, distant, mild, but there were huge chinks in her armour. Something in her, something that was beyond her control was so delighted to see him, so grateful that he had initiated a meeting at all, that she was unable to hold back, and immediately any ideas about being cool to him dissolved and the meeting, from her side, was as affectionate, as loving, as a father could wish.

Washing her hands in ice cold water, Nell thought back to these meetings. She knew that Fisher had a powerful effect on her, that the things he did and said were closely linked to her confidence and she resented herself for this weakness. But there it was, stronger than any rational decision she could make. Nell felt unsuppressable feelings for this person even if he had treated her roughly, never especially taken her age or her desires or her temperament into account. It was lack of willpower that made her cave in to him, she felt. She ought to try harder.

After their lunch Nell took a train back from Paddington so that she could attend a lecture being given by a distinguished, prize-winning American writer, whom both she and Marnie passionately and separately admired. The talk was held in one of the university's grand and central buildings and was attended by 2,000 people. The great man himself was older and stouter than Nell had expected, and the subject which seemed to fire him up most was the over-production, the over-processing of information, the chief culprits being newspapers.

However intelligently and articulately this personal grouse was voiced, Nell could not help herself thinking that this was not a million miles from what a boring person on a bus would say, and this depressed her. Marnie would never say anything so banal, she thought to herself, not that he wasn't interested in everyday things. In fact, Marnie loved ordinary pieces of odd knowledge. He admired the moment in a poem by Keats when the heroine's lover advises her to put on 'warm clothing' before escaping into the enchanted night. In a class he had given on the short story that Nell had attended, he had drawn their attention to a moment in a Saul Bellow novella when a character distinguishes himself by taking the distraught heroine's children to Burger King rather than any other hamburger outlet, because at Burger King, they flame-grill rather than fry the patties (more healthy). 'Now,' said Marnie, 'what comparable British writer, writing today (not of course that there is one) would have that sort of information at his fingertips?'

After the lecture, as the audience spilled out into the street, Nell caught sight of Helen and Robbie sloping off together to the bar of the Northgate Hotel. She followed them in there; Helen, as always was carting a large bag of library books over one shoulder. Lingering in the doorway, Nell watched Helen prop up the bag on an armchair covered in buttoned maroon cloth and sit down at a small square table; Robbie, cross-legged, was seated diagonally opposite from her, scribbling some notes into an exercise book.

'Hello, there,' Nell said.

'Nell,' Robbie sprang to his feet. 'Haven't seen you for ages. How have you been?'

'I've been in London,' she said. 'Went to see my dad.'

'How did that go?' Robbie said.

'It was OK. We went to an Italian restaurant.'

'Is he just over for the weekend?'

'No, it seems he's moving back. He's come over to get a place to live sorted out.'

'How do you feel about that?'

'I don't really know, to be honest with you. I've got so much on my mind at the moment.'

'What like?'

'Oh, I don't know, everything really. Rob?'

'Yeah?'

'You couldn't get me a Bloody Mary, could you?'

'Of course. D'you fancy one, Hell?'

'Yeah, great.'

Robbie went over to the bar. Quite a crowd had assembled whilst they had been talking.

'How are things?' Helen said to Nell.

'Yeah, not bad.'

'Are you coming to the Keats lecture tomorrow?'

'What time is it?'

'Two.'

'I've got to see someone in hospital then.'

'Nothing serious, I hope?'

'No, I don't think so.'

'Well, you're welcome to see my notes if you want.'

'Thanks.'

Robbie waved to them from the bar. Helen smiled. Finally he had got the attention of the barman.

'So what's been going on round here lately? Any gossip? You and Robbie . . . ?'

'Oh, no,' Helen said. 'Let me think. No, there's nothing new. I guess you know about Olivia Bayley?'

'No, what? Has she won Miss World?'

'No, she's pregnant.'

'No!'

'It's true, honestly. I can't say I'm all that surprised. You know what she's like.'

'I suppose so,' Nell shrugged her shoulders.

'Anyway,' Helen continued, 'you'll never guess who the father is?'

'I've no idea. A film star? A local trillionaire? Prince Edward?'

'No. Think again. It is guessable.'

'I can't think. I give up.'

'It's someone we both know.'

'Robbie Spittle. Give up. Tell me.'

'Bill Marnie.'

In a split second all the colour drained from Nell's face. 'Who told you that?'

'Had it from the horse's mouth.'

'Marnie told you?'

'Livvy broke down on me and Lisa after the class on Friday.'

'What did she say, exactly?'

'That she's pregnant and that Bill Marnie is the father. I don't think she's going to have the baby, though. She's not sure.'

'Does Marnie know?'

'Apparently she told him last week, but she hasn't heard a word from him since. He seems to have disappeared. Typical. I haven't seen him for days. Have you?'

When Robbie returned and put their three blood-red drinks on the table, he found Helen standing up and calling Nell's name. 'Are you all right? Are you OK?' Nell's eyes were closed and she had slumped back into her chair.

'Nell? Nell?' Robbie shook her arm and tried to lift the lids of her eyes. He ran to the bar. 'Can you call an ambulance?'

But long before the ambulance arrived, Nell came to. Slowly and shakily Robbie walked her back to college, put her to bed and went to sleep in the armchair in the corner of her room. Helen had gone back to the library, stinging from Robbie's attack. 'You said you'd let me tell her you spiteful bitch,' he had shouted, and it was all he could do not to slap her face.

To try to talk to Nell around this time was like

attempting conversation with someone who was being eaten by a shark. Whatever you might have to offer – well-chosen words, canny anecdotes, chat, any verbal booby prize – was *so* irrelevant that it made you feel instantly ridiculous and somehow cruel. Sometimes when you spoke to Nell, her features would clench together and appear to gather in the centre of her face, where they would fix into a violent wince that would hold until finally the need to breathe would force the muscles to relax. This raised the possibility that addressing her at all was causing additional strain. But it was arrogance even to consider that your words could be anything more than ineffectual. Her eyes often closed for as long as half a minute at a time while she spoke and as she did not alter her tone or refer to it in her speech in any way you could only guess that she had not noticed. She could not stay still for a moment, constantly shifting her weight from side to side if she stood and when she sat down she would busy herself with scratching at her forearms, which grew red and laced with tiny weals, or she would prize non-existent dirt from under her fingernails with any sharp implement to hand. Now and then she would scrape her hair back and fasten it with an elastic band that she generally wore on her wrist, only to undo it again seconds later but roughly so that small clumps of hair were torn out with the rubber each time.

You bumped into her in town walking the streets keeping very close to the inside edge of the pavement, her shoulder occasionally brushing against a bit of brick or shop front or stone wall and if you walked along with her for a while she'd grip onto you, often clutching both arms tightly – she said this was to prevent her from crashing herself into the traffic.

It was impossible to know what to do for the best. You could decide to refer to past events but something about her manner forbade you to do so. When it was time to go, your leaving was so painful to her that it might have been better not to have come round at all. She did odd things to try to get you to stay. She'd talk very quickly so that you could not physically get the words in. She'd give you taxi money so that you would prolong your visit. She would stand at the threshold whispering something under her breath with her fingers crossed, and if you listened hard to the low hissing you could just make out the same word over and over again, 'Please . . . Please . . . '

Often her friends would end up staying the night in the armchair or on the floor and very occasionally she persuaded new people to come back with her. She felt the lure of broken-down men at this time and would sit in pubs and cafés late into the night listening to the tragic lives of poor, weakened souls, who were worn down to less than a shadow. One evening, a man she had met in an out-of-the-way pub on one of her interminable walks offered to see her home and she had propped him up as they slowly walked the two miles back to college. He had fallen asleep the moment he had sat down on her bed, but had woken abruptly, anticipating romance, and had left in the middle of the night when she started shaking and screaming uncontrollably at his tentative advances. She had hoped they would just fall asleep together, head to toe in all their clothes.

She wanted people to come and see her all the time, but if you were ten minutes later arriving than you had said you would be she would be near-hysterical with worry and fear that you had met with an accident; or she would be furious, and your being late, even if you had the best of reasons, became not mere accident or thoughtlessness but a wish to humiliate her, as sharp and deliberate as if you had spat hard in her face. Yet she was always offering presents to the people who came to see her, books and clothes and other little gifts which she would press her guests to accept. She made sure there were delicious things to eat in the fridge, strangely festive foodstuffs: cream horns, slices of pink roast beef from the delicatessen on the high street, passion fruit designed to make the act of visiting her less tedious.

She occasionally attended lectures, everyone said it was important not to let her college work go, so she would stand at the back of the huge lecture theatres in the English faculty building with silent tears running down her face, trying and failing to write down every single word that the lecturer was saying, and the ink mingling with the crying so that even the notes themselves, crammed and floating between the lines of the narrow feint on the page, looked infinitely sad. Usually one of her friends would see her and come and stand by her side, loosening the pen from the hand that was writing so furiously and comforting her with wiping and stroking. She would turn up for tutorials (Marnie had taken a leave of absence and the head of department now took care of her year) so vague and with so many pages of unfathomable, loopy writing, that her teachers, sensing something was wrong, would offer to read her essays afterwards and try to engage her instead in general conversation on the books she was studying. When this failed they would read to her from rare works of criticism they esteemed or otherwise from the relevant novels and poems themselves. They did not think her behaviour especially odd. It was inevitably some sort of disastrous romantic attachment, Nell being a sensitive, ardent girl of that type. They had seen it a thousand times before, the temporary despairings of young women interfering with their academic work. Evidently her situation was extremely pressing, but if it had been anything else, anything more serious than love longings that afflicted her, she would undoubtedly have given a name to it. Serious female students would tell you frankly that their parents were divorcing or if there had been a bereavement or other family problems which were making demands on their thinking, but distress over a love affair seemed frivolous in the girls' eyes, and therefore undeserving of sympathy.

Throughout this unhurried time an awareness in Nell of what exactly had happened went missing. All she knew was that something very acute had taken place. It was not quite clear in her mind that this grave thing affected her specifically; she knew there had been a disaster all right, but it might have been of a more general nature – a local tragedy, children abducted, the murder of a young mother, the death of a member of her family. Words were hopeless but physical things, letting her hold on to you, stroking the back of her hands, smoothing her hair, did seem to soothe her a little. She'd even let you tuck her into bed, shaking, in the afternoons. She could not really sleep or eat. After a few days she stopped using her bed at night and would try out different sleeping places, under the table or in the small hollow between the chair and the picture window in her room, on the floor in the bathroom parallel to the deep white bath. She grew thinner. Her body became too small for her head, the large-boned face looked odd, just supported by its tiny neck as if the perspective had been done all wrong.

This period of shock lasted for eighteen days, then the wave of grief broke. Marnie was gone. The tragedy was personal to her. She loved him more than she could possibly say. She no longer mattered to the person who mattered to her most of all.

Chapter 12

It was Robbie who saw her through this time. Most mornings he would come and work in her room, bringing her fruit and milk and delicious items of high nutritious value to tempt her appetite and help restore her health.

Letters soon started arriving from Marnie, one or two pale blue envelopes a week, and though Nell intended to deal with them, she could not quite bring herself to read their contents, and so they formed a neat little stack on her desk. Robbie must have contacted Nell's mother, because on three occasions she came to visit Nell and sat with her all day, hand in hand, saying hardly anything at all, with tears dripping down her chin onto Nell's bedspread. Someone must have spoken to Laura's mother also, because she seemed to know something of what had happened and drove down in her shiny red car to take Nell out to lunch. But Nell couldn't think of a single word to say to her and they ended up talking about furnishing fabrics and department stores.

Only Laura's frequent visits to Nell were a success, the two girls lying head to toe in Nell's bed and talking for hours about when they were young. Laura was getting married in the summer but she was keeping it under her hat for the time being, waiting for the right moment to let her old friend know. After a while a letter came from Olivia Bayley.

Dear Nell,

I'm probably the last person in the world you want to hear from right now but I had to write and let you know that I spent exactly one night with Marnie, when I was feeling v. depressed and he was drunk, and it meant nothing to either of us. I have decided not to keep the baby. Please believe me when I say I had absolutely no idea that the two of you were together and if I had known I would not have slept with him in a million years. Please know how sorry I am and how much I care for you. With love, Olivia.

Nell read it, shrugged her shoulders and handed it to Robbie. 'She didn't know, Nell. You must believe her. I was the only person in college who knew. You were both so careful.'

'It doesn't matter if she knew or not.'

End of term exams came and went. Robbie arranged with the head of department for Nell to take the papers in a small room with a girl who had brittle diabetes and the college nurse on hand. Tea and biscuits were brought in at half time. Nell muddled through, achieving a perfectly respectable result, and although it saddened her not to have performed to her best ability, she accepted it as a fact of this part of her life. Her twentieth birthday fell on the last day of term. Apart from a cheque for £5,000 from her father, which came by registered post, the day passed uneventfully. She spent the evening with Robbie in a gay pub near college drinking cider and eating roast chicken crisps, despite all his efforts to tempt her out to somewhere more festive.

Nell returned to London for the holidays to be greeted by a mother riddled with anxiety. Nell's rapid loss of weight was her mother's first concern and she spent much time preparing rich foods high in fat and protein in order to put some meat on her daughter's bones. She was relieved that Nell put up no resistance to her efforts, but meekly finished the creamy soups, oily stews and sticky puddings set before her. That Nell was often sick after these meals her mother didn't know. Having eaten next to nothing for three weeks, this sort of diet was too great a shock to her system. Her mother attended to her in other ways, taking care not to do anything that might surprise her, avoiding sudden moves and unpredictable behaviour, taking care not to expose her daughter to anything that might trouble her further. She left the house infrequently, but when she did have to go out she would pick up small presents for her daughter on her travels, a pack of fluorescent felt pens, some floral notelets, a couple of vests. Nell, for her part, threw herself into her work, setting herself the target of reading for ten hours a day, and in this way she managed to kill the days without too many distressing thoughts. The dull, thudding ache inside her did not diminish, but she acclimatized herself to it, carried herself onwards avoiding the urge to probe the nooks and crannies of her broken heart.

When she wasn't reading or eating, Nell slept. She found sleeping easy at this time. In fact, it was difficult to stay awake, but she clung fiercely to her routine, rising at seven-thirty every day, making sure she was well into her book by nine.

On her fourth night at home, just as she was getting ready for bed at ten o'clock, her mother knocked on her door. 'Come in,' Nell said drowsily.

'How you feeling darling?'

'Sleepy.'

'I won't be a minute. I just wanted to say a couple of things.'

'OK. I can't promise to stay awake, though.'

'I've just been thinking. I don't know. I was just thinking about you and Marnie. I mean what if, have you thought of going to see him at all, just to talk, just to have a go at sorting things out. It seems to me that you must have a lot to say to each other, and if you won't answer his letters, or speak to him, I don't know. I wouldn't want you to do anything to make yourself worse. It would probably be painful, but wouldn't you like to hear him explain his side of things? I mean, if he's truly sorry . . . I mean, I don't want to make excuses, but when people are ill, I mean as ill as that, they can do all sorts of things that they wouldn't dream of doing, you know, when they're well.'

'I can't . . . ' Nell said distantly, almost as if she were the only person in the room. 'I feel like he's smashed me up. I can't think of him as a friend any more. I mean that's just not what friends do. I was completely stupid to get so involved. I know it's my fault. It's wrong to give someone your heart like that, because they . . . they just drop it. Every time. I mean I could never . . . I wouldn't dream of making someone like me and then smash it all up as if they were nothing, less than a beetle. And I would have looked after him. I would have tried to find out about his illness, I don't know, studied about it, done a course or something so I could have cared for him properly. I just about could have done it. You didn't see what he was like in hospital, Mum, but it was really frightening. He didn't recognize me. He looked at me as if he hated me. But I think I could just about have coped, could have muddled through somehow, but I would have had to leave college. It would have been like a full-time job, I wouldn't really have had time for anything else . . . But if he doesn't even want me? If he could do something like that? I mean I don't think we've really . . . I don't know. Maybe I'll feel differently in a few weeks. But . . . I doubt it. I can't . . . There's only so much. You know . . . I mean, I'm only human.'

'I know, darling. I know. It makes total sense what you say. I shouldn't have said anything.'

'I've been a complete fool, haven't I?'

'You absolutely have not. You acted in good faith.'

Her mother's face was wet with tears. She was bringing to mind her own sadnesses. 'You loved someone with all your heart. There's absolutely nothing wrong with that. That's what hearts are for.'

After a week of this, a letter arrived from her father. He had returned from America and was now newly installed in London. Inside the letter was a printed change of address card and a note asking her to come and see him on the following Wednesday at five at the new house.

When the day came Nell took a bus to her father's. She felt little anxiety about the meeting, almost welcoming it as a distraction from sharper thoughts and from her reading, which no longer seemed a comfort and had begun to be a form of persecution to her, for to read about people happy or unhappy in love filled her with fresh despair. At these moments her mouth, which was wet from catching dribbled tears, would open as wide as it could, as if preparing to scream, but no sound would be emitted. Instead she would have difficulty finding her breath, and in the attempt to exhale, something inside her throat would grow so taut that only muffled choking coughs would come. It became one of her greatest fears that she would choke to death. It was something she often dreamed of, a long, tortured self-strangulation, draining the very last drop of colour from her face.

Nell's mother had encouraged her daughter to dress nicely for the visit to her father's house and when Nell had failed to respond, the older woman had picked out some of Nell's clothes and laid them out on her bed: a thin cotton long-sleeved T-shirt, a soft grey cardigan, a short black wool skirt with buttons down the front, her mother's best coat. Nell put the clothing on carefully, but it was only as she was about to leave the house that her mother noticed that the garments were hanging oddly askew, and realized that her daugther had not had the heart to do up any of her buttons. She performed this small task for her daughter, who seemed to be in such an abstract frame of mind that she might have easily made the mistake of going out in no clothes at all.

'Look, Nell, I think I'll take you there, if you don't mind. I'd quite like a look round the shops and then maybe we could have a cup of coffee somewhere afterwards. It doesn't seem a terribly good idea, you going alone.'

'Honestly, I'll be fine,' Nell said.

'Are you sure?'

'I'm not ill, Mum.'

'You do feel well enough to go on your own?'

'I'll be fine.'

'Well, if you're sure.' Nell's mother folded her daughter in an embrace, trying to send some cheer and strength from her own frame into that of her child. Nell's body was limp and bony in her arms.

'I'll see you later then.'

'Yes, see you later, darling.'

Fisher's new house was tall and thin. Fisher himself was standing outside on the doorstep when Nell appeared.

'How lovely to see you,' he said, holding out an arm to his daughter. He pulled her sharply towards him and kissed both her cheeks. 'Your mother tells me you've been having an awful time.'

Nell nodded and bit her lip. 'She told me about it on the telephone.' Nell nodded again. She would not meet her father's eyes. He motioned with his arm for her to enter the house and followed behind her. She felt the flat of his hand, guiding her lightly, against her back. From the hall she could hear that outside it had started to rain. The rain fell heavily. Fisher led her into the kitchen. It was a huge white L-shaped room with a ceiling that must have been two and a half times as high as he was. The floor was white; French windows gave onto a mysterious-looking garden, where bamboos grew and wild roses and a small apple tree.

They sat down at a large round table near the doors to the garden. Fisher got up, poured some Evian into a gleaming stainless steel kettle and put it on to boil. He sat down again.

'So you're back for good, then,' Nell said.

'That's right. I had certain ideas about America. You can do things there you can't do here, but it's never going to feel like home. You've never been there, have you?'

'No.'

'I did hope you'd come and stay and,' he paused, 'I hope you'll come and stay here often. There are four bedrooms.'

Nell said nothing. She had found an ancient piece of

tissue in her skirt pocket and was twisting it into a tight cone.

There was a piercing sound of whistling and Fisher got up to take the kettle off the stove. He put a tea pot and some very delicate blue and white cups and saucers on a dark tray and brought it over to Nell. She poured out two cups.

'Lovely china,' she said.

'It's good, isn't it? I asked the man in the shop how much it was, knowing it would be a lot because I know a bit about what things cost, and it was actually three times as much as I'd thought.'

'But you bought it anyway.'

Fisher smiled and took a sip of his tea . He drank it black. Nell did too.

'Do you think you'll take the rest of the year off?'

'I don't know. I hadn't really thought.'

'It might be an idea.'

'I don't know.'

Fisher cleared his throat. 'It's extremely unfortunate . . . ' he stopped and began again. 'I'm extremely sorry that you've had to experience something like this. Your mother says that your friend has had a breakdown . . . and I thought you might like to ask me, I mean obviously, from a professional point of view, if you'd like me to explain how these things often seem to work, or . . . how they can affect the behaviour and so on . . . Your mother's anxious . . .'

'It's all right,' Nell said.

But Fisher was undeterred. 'Your mother's anxious

that this, that what has happened, may have broken you in some way. That you have taken certain things as if they were directed against you when in fact, the events aren't to do with you in the least as far as I can make out from the little I've been told. I myself feel that you've had an absolutely horrible shock and that you're going to feel pretty rotten for quite some time, but that eventually . . . ' Fisher stopped talking. After a while he said, 'Anyway I've got something for you.' He handed Nell a Harrods carrier bag in which there was a box containing a camera with two lenses, one long and one short, and three rolls of film. 'Thank you very much,' she whispered. 'That's really kind. I haven't got a good camera. What a good idea.'

'Not at all. Not at all.'

They were silent for a while. Nell sipped her tea, still avoiding her father's gaze. 'I do think it'll probably be all right—' but the end of the word rebelled against itself, collapsed into a wet cough and then a sob and then hot silent tears. Nell opened her mouth wide, tipped back her head and closed her eyes tightly inwards on her grief. After a few seconds she felt a large hand on her left shoulder. '*Courage.*' She heard the two soft syllables over her head and she opened her eyes to see her father's dark-suited figure towering above her, his eyes smiling down at her trouble and the silence broke and she cried towards him with all her might.